The Carved Box

by Gillian Chan

KGL

Kids Can Press

Kids Can Press acknowledges the financial support of the Ontario Arts Council, the Canada Council for the Arts and the Government of Canada, through the BPIDP, for our publishing activity.

The author also wishes to acknowledge the financial support of the Ontario Arts Council in the writing of this novel.

ONTARIO ARTS COUNCIL
CONSEIL DES ARTS DE L'ONTARIO

Published in Canada by
Kids Can Press Ltd.
29 Birch Avenue
Toronto, ON M4V 1E2

Published in the U.S. by
Kids Can Press Ltd.
2250 Military Road
Tonawanda, NY 14150

Edited by Charis Wahl
Cover designed by Marie Bartholomew
Interior designed by Stacie Bowes
Printed and bound in Canada

CM 01 0 9 8 7 6 5 4 3 2 1
CM PA 01 0 9 8 7 6 5 4 3 2 1

Canadian Cataloguing in Publication Data

Chan, Gillian
   The carved box

ISBN 1-55074-895-5 (bound)   ISBN 1-55337-016-3 (pbk.)

I. Title.

PS8555.H39243C37 2001   jC813'.54   C00-932862-9
PZ7.C42Ca 2001

Kids Can Press is a Nelvana company

This book is for Anne Gray,
a true friend, who always believed
in Callum and Dog.

Prologue

I have it! I have it! The words of his triumph bounced and rattled in his head as he crashed through the thick undergrowth. Risking a look back over one shoulder, he saw nothing save the movement of the leaves and fern fronds jostled by his headlong passage.

He slowed down, his feet now moving in a fast trot. A smile twisted his features as he thought of her. She had been so convinced of her righteousness, of her strength, that she had dared to challenge him, her own brother, with whom she had shared her every breath since she was born a scant seven minutes after him. She had denounced him to the Council, accused him of misusing the power.

He had borne their disapproval, had bowed his head in mock shame while the old men had made their windy speeches, their wrinkled mouths savoring his humiliation. Glancing sideways, he had been able to see her, sitting so still next to their grandfather, another one who was blind to the power they had, the gift they had been given. There was no doubt that the old fool would back her; he had always revered tradition, and he would make sure that control of the family would pass to her on his own death. The man knew that he was the more worthy, that he could raise them all to the status of gods, if only they would trust him, let him take risks. He had looked down at his sister again. She had her head bowed like his, her eyes fixed on her hands, her long fingers twisted and twined.

It was then that he had known what he must do. Now, after the long hours tracking her silently through the woods, watching her in the places she had thought secret and safe, he had done it. Never again would she be able to challenge or thwart him. And the old man, he would be easy meat without her youth and strength. The man's face twisted into a snarling grin as he remembered that day.

Mist still lay curled around the long houses as he entered the village. It would stay until the sun, just showing above the tips of the dark pines, was strong enough to burn it off. He saw no one, heard nothing, as he made his way to the center of the village, where there stood a small conical lean-to made out of branches. Once inside, he pulled its crude door shut behind him, immobilizing the latch with knotted deer sinew. Squatting on his haunches, he rested, allowing his eyes to adjust to the gloom. Then he began to scrabble at the soft earth of the floor.

"Hah!" His fingers found the package he had buried earlier.

Fumbling in his eagerness, he tugged at the covering of deerskin to reveal a wooden box, and underneath that its lid. For a moment, he hesitated, tracing the designs he had carved with such care on the lid. Shivering, he reached inside his shirt and drew out what he had plotted to gain. A stray beam of weak sunlight filtered through the branches, and the stuff that he held shimmered as he folded it into the box. He dropped the lid in place, muttering, his hands making strange sinuous movements above it. When he picked up the box and turned it, no line showed where lid and box met.

Outside there was a scuffling, a scratching at the door, and a dog whimpered. He rocked back on his heels and grinned, a grin that consumed his whole face.

Chapter One

Trees.

Callum had never seen so many trees.

As the bateau glided toward the shore, a solid wall of green loomed over it, swallowing up the bright sunlight.

Callum shivered, longing for the familiar, noisy streets of Edinburgh. The only sounds here were birdsongs and the splash of the oars as the boatman guided the boat to a makeshift dock that looked as if it might tumble into the water at any minute — an impression confirmed by the way it swayed when Callum stepped onto it and reached back to take his box.

"Is this it?" As soon as he spoke, Callum regretted the words.

"Not good enough for you, is it? I'd wager you were expecting something fancier." The man's voice was rough and his eyes were hard, lingering on Callum's clothes.

"N-no." Callum suddenly felt hot, was conscious of sweat trickling down his back under the heavy wool coat — one of Dr. Lennie's that his wife had insisted on cutting down for Callum.

She had shaken her head. "We cannae send you off to your uncle in Canada looking like a wee ragamuffin. John has no need of these" — she had indicated the pile of shirts and britches, topped off with the coat — "and it won't take but a few stitches to alter them to fit." Clicking her tongue as she had struggled to thread the needle, she'd continued, "I know your father was poorly for some time, but you look a real gowk with your arms and legs sticking out of your clothes."

Callum had tried to protest, to stop her from criticizing his father, but she didn't even appear to register that he had spoken. "If I'd had my way, we'd have spent some of the money your father's parishioners got together on outfitting you properly, but, oh no, Dr. Lennie wouldn't have it." She lowered her voice into a passable version of her husband's gruff tones. "Let's pay for his passage to Upper Canada, and let young Callum take anything that's left with him to give to his uncle."

Callum's hand sneaked into his britches' pocket, and he felt the comforting weight of several coppers and, most important of all, the two gold coins. He realized that the boatman was looking at him expectantly, waiting for him to say more. "I-I-I didn't know what to expect," he stuttered. "My uncle's letter said that I was to come to Coote's Paradise. I thought that was the name of the village or town he lived in, yet I see nothing but trees." Callum was unaware that his disdain showed clearly as he glanced around.

The boatman started to laugh, a deep but not unfriendly laugh. "Well, if you call a mill, an inn and a few scattered homesteads a village, then I suppose that's what we have here. What's your uncle's name, lad?"

"Rory MacBean."

"Oh, I know him, a big fellow, red hair like yours only fierier in color. Squatting out toward the other side of the valley."

Callum shrugged, not caring what the boatman thought or knew. He had his own picture of his uncle, one polished over the years until it glowed. "I've no met him. He's my mammie's brother." Callum was about to say more, to tell of how Rory came out to the Americas before Callum was even born, and how he fought in the war against the American rebels before bringing his family to Upper Canada, but he stopped himself. What business of this man was his family history, even though he claimed acquaintance with Callum's uncle? Even so, Callum couldn't help smiling, remembering how his mother's spirits rose whenever a letter came from "her Rory," how she read and reread them until the paper grew worn and thin. Those letters rested at the bottom of his box now, a tattered bundle, one of the few things of his mother's that he had left.

"Is he meeting you then?" The boatman was looking over his shoulder at the lake. The wind was rising and whitecaps were appearing on the water.

"No. I mean, I don't know." All the bitterness, fear and anger that Callum had been feeling since he left Scotland were welling up inside him, forming a tight knot, making it difficult to speak or even think. "He knows I'm coming. Dr. Lennie wrote him. He replied saying that extra hands were always of use on the land." A sour taste filled Callum's mouth. The land, what did he know of land? He'd spent all his life in the city, but after his father's death, everyone had been too busy trying to get a troublesome orphan off their hands. Not even Dr. Lennie, supposedly his father's best friend, had asked Callum what he wanted, even though Callum's father had always told him what a good scholar Callum was. When Callum had tried to describe his dreams of being a teacher or a lawyer, the doctor had laughed. "You've got to be practical, laddie. Your uncle's the only family you have who's willing to take you. If you stay here, the best I can do for you is to find you an apprenticeship, and, for a boy like you with your head full of fancy ideas, it'd be hard going to be fending for yourself so young."

"Ah, he's right there."

Callum shook his head, almost believing that he had said Dr. Lennie's words out loud and that the boatman was answering them.

"The best crop is children, that's what they say, and MacBean's are still young. Till they're grown, a boy of your age will be right handy, I reckon." A meaty finger pointed to a mere gap in the trees. "That path will take you to the inn. Either you'll find someone going out your uncle's way or they'll get word to him. I'd show you the path myself, but the weather looks like it's turning and I want to be on my way before it does."

Callum hefted his leather and wood box, feeling its weight bite into his shoulder. He hesitated, then lifted a hand in farewell, but said nothing when he realized that the boatman's head was down as he busied himself with casting off.

After the bright glare of the afternoon sunlight, it took several minutes before Callum's eyes adjusted to the cool gloom of the forest. The path, if it could be called that, was no more than a man's width, twisting through the trees. Brambles caught at Callum's legs, and more than once he wondered if he was heading in the right direction. He stared down at the soft ground, straining to see any sign of a footprint. A chill overtook him and a rustle in the bushes nearby caused him to stop, his eyes frantically searching for its source. He saw leaves moving as a creature ran, but he could not make out what it was. All he got was a sense of something dark, not caring what noise it made. Its size seemed to be that of a large dog. Unbidden, a name popped into his head, *Cu Sith*. He had been terrified when his mother told him stories of the *Cu Sith*, the fairy dog that haunted the forests of the Highlands, looking for unwary and foolish travelers. Did the Americas have such creatures? Callum was close to panic.

He could hear his mother's voice, the way in which it sank low and became husky whenever she told the old stories, almost as if she feared to speak them too loudly. His father's disapproval had been loud and snorting. "Fairy tales for weans!" he had called them, and Callum always knew that his lessons would be harder for a while, more rigorous, as if his father wished to purge him of such fancies by cramming Latin verbs and declensions into his head. In an attempt to calm himself, Callum drew on this memory, his lips mouthing Julius Caesar's words like a charm against fear. "Gallia in tres partes divisa est."

Callum's box was weighing heavier and heavier, but he forced himself to start moving his feet. Whatever the animal was, it seemed to be deliberately keeping pace with him, alongside the path, concealed in the thick undergrowth. Callum's fear increased until he felt he could hardly breathe. He realized that he had shut his eyes and was walking blind. Forcing himself to open them again, he caught a glimpse of thick, brindled gray fur. "Arma virumque, cano, Troiae qui primus ab oris ..." The familiar Latin words of the Virgil he'd studied so often did nothing to stop his heart racing, but when he spoke them aloud, they did at least drown out the rustling leaves. He concentrated on placing one foot methodically in front of the other, trying not to look anywhere but straight ahead. When he finally saw daylight as the trees thinned out, Callum started to run, disregarding the way the box bounced painfully, bruising his shoulder, until he found himself standing beside a rough-and-ready log building, facing what he supposed passed for a road in these parts, hard-packed dirt pocked with stumps of trees. Nothing followed him out from the trees, although he had the sense that something was lurking just out of sight, staring intently at him.

Shivering, Callum forced himself to square his shoulders and move forward. Now that he was out of the forest, he convinced himself that his fears were foolish — the product of an overactive imagination. That's what his father would have said, and such an imagination was not something to be cultivated.

The sun burned down fiercely and sweat soaked Callum's shirt. A sloping roof jutted out from the wall that faced the road, providing a measure of shade. Callum stepped under it and squawked in surprise as the ground seemed to move beneath his foot. His box slipped from his shoulder and landed with a thud on rough planking. Callum hardly had time to right himself when a tall, burly man came running from the building, his fists raised to strike. Callum flinched, covering his head with his hands.

"You varmint! You wicked beast! Tripping the young gentleman like that."

Callum stared, frozen in astonishment. A large black dog was the recipient of the blows and buffets he had feared. The dog did not whimper, but Callum heard a dull whumping sound each time the man's hands connected with its side.

"Sir. Sir!" When the man paid no heed to him, Callum got painfully to his feet, managing to place himself between the enraged man and the dog, but not before one of the man's fists landed on his already aching shoulder. "Your dog did nothing. It was I who caused it injury, for which I apologize. Please do not punish it any further." In his ears, his voice sounded high and shrill, like that of a petulant child.

The man stood breathing heavily, his face contorted with rage. Callum's knees felt weak as he saw the size of the man he had confronted with so little thought. Although Callum was tall for his fifteen years, this man peered down at him from what must have been near six-and-a-half feet of height. His shoulders were broad, his arms and hands roped with muscle. To add to his fearsome aspect, he had marks on his face the like of which Callum had never seen — rows of dots, arranged in a pattern of angles and lines, that ran along his cheekbones before disappearing into his thick black hair. Frightened that he might give offense by staring so, Callum dropped to his knees once more, busying himself with examining the dog and avoiding the man's stare.

Like its master, the dog was powerful in build, with long, heavy bones that hinted at great strength. As Callum ran his hands over its fur, his fingers encountered burrs, knotted lumps and what felt like scabs and welts. Not making a sound, the dog raised its head and looked steadily at Callum, its large dark eyes locking on to his green ones. Callum had the sensation that he was falling, of losing himself in something he did not understand. He shivered and forced himself to look away, although it took all his will to do so.

"Let me help you up, young sir." For a moment, Callum wondered who it was who spoke with such a calm and determinedly pleasant voice. He risked a glance at the man. His face, although still reddened by his anger, had been rearranged in the semblance of a smile. He was extending his hand to Callum, who was almost lifted off his feet when he took it. A huge arm encircled Callum's shoulders and he found himself being shepherded inside the building, the man talking all the while. "Come into the inn and let me buy you some ale. It's the least I can do after your upset. By your clothes and your box, you've been traveling long and hard, and a drink will be welcome, will it not?"

At the mention of his box, Callum looked around for it, only to see it firmly tucked beneath his new friend's other arm. The dog got slowly to its feet and silently followed them into the inn.

Almost as if he was dealing with a little child, the man helped Callum to a seat on a wooden settle by an empty fireplace, carefully placing Callum's box on the floor at his feet. The dog took up a position alongside the settle, lying down on the hard-packed dirt floor and resting its head on its front paws.

His head whirling with all that had happened — the beast in the forest, his fall and the puzzling behavior of the dog's owner — Callum barely managed to stutter out a shaky "Y-y-yes" when asked if he would indeed take some ale. While his new-found companion turned to the high counter of the bar, Callum took the opportunity to look around him. Tables, benches and the settle were arranged around a surprisingly spacious room. A little light came in through the open door and some small windows cut in the log walls and covered with oiled paper. Unlike the tavern at which he'd stayed in York while waiting for passage down the lake to Coote's Paradise, this place at least appeared clean. There was no sawdust clotted with tobacco juice or morsels of stale food here. The dirt floor had been swept and sprinkled with water. Hams and bunches of drying herbs hung from the low ceiling, giving the place a fresh and pleasant smell that made Callum think of his mother's kitchen before she became ill the last time. He swallowed hard, fighting back the wave of sadness that came with the memory, when he suddenly had the feeling he was being closely observed.

Callum tried to locate the watcher, but, apart from the innkeeper and the dog's owner, who were both intent on the purchase of ale, there was no one else in the place. He shuddered, remembering how Annie MacBean, his mother's old nurse, had said that such feelings were the wee folk making themselves known. A low sound, between a bark and a whimper, drew his attention to the dog and he realized he had found his observer. The dog was staring fixedly at Callum and, almost against his will, he found himself stroking it. As he caressed its ears, the dog leaned its head into Callum's hand, and he felt a need to reassure it, talking softly so that no one would hear him and think him foolish. "You're a fine animal. I'll not let anyone hurt you." Callum closed his eyes, feeling the thick fur beneath his fingers, trying to avoid any of the dog's old hurts. "By the looks of things, you havnae had it easy." He sighed, thinking of how that made them a pair. How in the space of two years, his life had changed so much and here he was now, in a strange land, dependent on the kindness of people he had never met.

"So, you've made friends with Bess, have you?"

Callum was startled out of his thoughts as a clay mug of ale was thrust in front of him.

"A tricky beast." The man shook his head. "Causing trouble one minute and then giving you looks with those sad eyes. Always getting round people. But I know how to keep her in line." With that, he raised his hand as if to strike the dog once more.

Callum tensed, knowing only that the dog aroused some strange protective instinct in him and that he would not allow her to be hurt further, no matter what.

Laughing, the man lowered his hand and sat down. "She's done it to you, hasn't she? You were going to try and stop me." He looked long and hard at Callum with eyes the color of wet slate. "So, am I right about the traveling?"

Callum's nerves were a jangle. Too many strange things were happening — the stranger's moods changed too quickly, and he was too interested in Callum. Callum tried to think of a way of avoiding the question without seeming rude or provoking yet another sudden bout of temper. A steady pressure against his leg caused him to look down. Hidden from her master, the dog was now sitting up, leaning her not inconsiderable weight on Callum's leg. He reached down and let his hand rest on her head, thankful for the idea it gave him of how to deflect the man's interest.

"Your dog, sir, what kind might she be? I've not seen her like before."

"Bess? She's a rare kind of dog." The man's eyes glittered. To Callum it seemed he was trying hard not to laugh. "As to exactly what kind, that I couldn't say. Some have said that she puts them in mind of those swimming dogs from Newfoundland. That might be — she has a powerful liking for water." Taking a swig of his ale, the man leaned over the table, his face coming close to Callum's. "Have you taken a fancy to her then, young gentleman?" These words were delivered in almost a singsong, wheedling way.

Callum leaned as far back as the unyielding settle would allow. "She's a fine animal."

"Well, maybe I'll tell you the really odd thing about her, then." With that, the man fumbled inside his shirt and pulled out a box, which he slapped down upon the table, making the innkeeper turn their way.

Callum felt rather than saw the dog tense. Her body became still, and Callum heard a growl so low that he felt it almost as a vibration.

About the size of a small Bible, the box lay on the table in front of Callum. He picked it up, surprised by its weight, which seemed too great for its size. He turned it over and over in his hands, feeling with his fingertips. A series of snakelike curves had been carved into the wood. They teased and tricked the fingers into following them, always leading away from what Callum felt should be the edges of the lid. Resisting the pull of the lines, he used his thumbnail to try to lever up the lid.

"Got you puzzled, eh?" The man took the box from Callum's hand and tried to open the lid, too. "See. It doesn't open. You know what? As long as you keep this box sealed like this, Bess is bound to be your faithful servant. If you should break it open though, then ..." The man looked calculatingly at Callum. "Listen to me, here I am talking like Bess belonged to you!" He paused, clapped his hand dramatically to his forehead as if an idea had just occurred to him. "A dog is an asset to any man. You wouldn't be interested in buying her, would you?"

Callum's mind said no, but he was shocked to hear himself say, "I might be."

"No, I wasn't really thinking." The man stood up to leave. "It's not right. Bess is my dog." He grinned down at the dog, a grin that looked almost like a snarl. "She's been mine for nigh on ten years." He shook his head and, almost as if he was talking to himself, said, "There's no denying that she's a tie, though. I always have to be on my guard against her tricky ways." He straightened up. "No, I'll not be parted from her." With that, he clicked his tongue and started for the door.

Her eyes never leaving Callum's face, the dog rose to her feet and reluctantly followed her master.

"Wait! I've two gold sovereigns." As the words came out of his mouth, Callum had the strange sensation that someone else was speaking.

"Done!"

In seconds, Callum was relieved of his money and the man was out the door, tossing the weird box to Callum, who instinctively caught it before it could hit the table.

The dog had halted in mid-stride and, as Callum caught the box, she turned, walked toward Callum and sat down beside him.

Callum's head was spinning. He put a shaky hand into his pocket and pulled out his depleted store of money. The few coppers looked dull and tarnished as he laid them carefully on the table.

"Did I hear aright?" The innkeeper had come out from behind his counter and was standing over Callum. "You've bought that dog?" He shook his head. "That fellow's been hanging round the place for the last week. Can't say I liked the look of him." He paused. "Threw him out once, when he pestered old Sam Waters about buying the dog." Looking Callum up and down, he said, "Can't believe anyone would fall for his stories. How much did you pay for that half-starved creature?"

Callum stiffened and stood up, trying to stare the innkeeper down. In his iciest tone, he said, "That, sir, is my business alone."

"Too much, then." The innkeeper's smile faded, and his voice was tightly controlled when he continued. "If I am not intruding on your privacy, might I ask your name and business here? I've had enough trouble from that fellow to last me a while and I'll not be putting up with any more."

Callum bristled at the innkeeper's tone. He said, "I've come from Scotland to join my uncle who's farming hereabouts. I'll thank you for directions and then I'll leave, for I'll not stay anyplace where I am not welcome nor treated with common courtesy."

To Callum's surprise, the innkeeper began to laugh. He laughed so much that his face turned red, and he sat down heavily on the settle, causing the dog to move closer to Callum's leg.

Between cackles, he forced out, "You must be Rory MacBean's boy — the same red hair, the same stiff-necked pride. He said he was expecting a nephew from the Old Country. How did he put it? 'A whey-faced city boy who probably won't know one end of a cow from the other.' Is that a fair description of yourself?"

Callum felt as if his blood had turned to ice water. Even though he had hated coming here, he had always assumed he would have a welcome, if only for his mother's sake. Rory had never let her down, she'd told Callum, not even when the rest of her family would have nothing to do with her after her marriage to Callum's father, a Protestant and, worst of all, a minister. Rory had always written, even after he sailed for America with a kinsman two years before the outbreak of the war.

Callum's fingers found the reassuring warmth of the dog's fur. When he spoke, he was pleased that his voice did not betray his feelings. "It may well be, sir. But back home, working with animals is not a skill that a gentleman is expected to possess!"

Slapping his thigh and laughing again, the innkeeper said, "Well, my fine young gentleman, you have a lot to learn about life here. I'd like to be around as your uncle teaches you a few lessons." He stood up and moved toward the open door. "As to how to get to Rory's place, you're in luck, boy. Your uncle took his cart over to the Masons' farm to pick up a barrel that Josh Mason made for him. He'll be passing by here on his way home, in about half an hour's time by my reckoning, and I've never known him not to stop for an ale!" He looked back to where Callum stood. "You can either wait outside or" — and he smiled here — "if you've the money left, I'll set you up with bread, cheese and something to wash it down."

Callum's mouth filled with saliva at the thought of food. He had had nothing to eat since early morning, and then only a stale pie he had bought the night before. He shook his head. "I'll wait outside," he said and pushed past the man, the dog following closely at his heels. Over his shoulder, he couldn't resist adding, "That is, if you don't charge for the use of your shade."

A soft snort made Callum turn back. The innkeeper's face was expressionless, but his voice was less brusque when he spoke. "There's a well out back. Help yourself to what you need, and there's an old crock there you can use to give the dog a drink. Her last master was less than careful about such things."

The well water was cool, slipping easily down Callum's dry throat. He grappled the leather bucket up and poured some out for the dog, who lapped it up quickly and then looked beseechingly for more. Callum squatted beside her as he poured out a second bowl, and stroked the dog's dusty fur. "A good bath is what you need. You're even dirtier than me and that's saying something." Rocking back on his heels, Callum thought for a moment. Then he dipped his hands into the bucket, dashing the remaining water onto his face and hair. "That'll have to do for now, though. Mebbe when we get to my uncle's farm we can get ourselves clean."

The dog looked at him, her brown eyes serious, and let loose a small wuff.

"It's strange," Callum said, "but I'd swear you understand what I'm saying. That sounded suspiciously like an agreement. Well, that's good, because we're landed with each other now." He sighed. "I'm going to have to do some explaining when my Uncle Rory comes, but if what my mammie said was true — how he had a soft and tender heart for animals — all should be well."

Almost as if in response to Callum's words, the rattle of wheels on the rutted road could be heard in the distance. Callum jumped to his feet, his heart beating wildly. The water that had been so cool on his face now felt clammy. He picked up his box, felt inside his coat for the smaller box, and made his way to the front of the inn, only remembering about the dog as he rounded the corner. He need not have worried. The dog was walking a few paces behind him, as if an invisible string tied them together.

A cloud of dust almost obscured the cart and driver, but even if there had not been a barrel in the back, Callum would have known that this was Rory MacBean, so often had his mother described her younger brother. Her eyes always looked misty, tears threatening, and her voice took on a singsong lilt. "Aye, Rory was a fine-looking fellow. Tall and strong like a young tree. Hair so red it looked like it was afire. Blue, blue eyes like ice, but for all that, he had a gentle manner about him. Apart from your eyes, Callum, you favor him a lot. Those you got from your da."

Callum felt himself standing straighter, hoping that his uncle would recognize him without anything being said, that he would leap down from the cart and hold him tight, saying that he would have known Ailsa's son anywhere, that Callum was home now.

"Eh, Rory!" the innkeeper's voice rang out from behind Callum. "I've got your nephew here, and the bloody young fool's let himself be rooked out of his money already!"

Chapter Two

Rory MacBean drew his cart to a halt. Callum's blood pounded in his head as he stared at his uncle, watching for his reaction to the innkeeper's jeering words. When he finally did move, MacBean jumped lightly down from the cart and tied the oxen's reins to a post before turning to face Callum.

Callum could not meet his uncle's eyes and stared down at the dog, who was looking up at him.

"So, nephew. You made the long journey safely." MacBean's voice was even in tone, lacking the anger Callum had been expecting. He noticed that his uncle kept his eyes on the innkeeper as he spoke, seeming to take his time in choosing his words. "Your father's friend gave me no notice of when you would leave Scotland, only that you would be coming before the summer was out."

As Callum let out a great sigh, he realized he had been holding his breath. He felt himself begin to relax and he took his first good look at the man who was now his guardian. Standing more than six feet in height, Rory MacBean was an impressive sight.

Callum's mother had described him as being like a young tree, but time and hard work had seasoned him to a great oak, solid and strong. His red hair still burned fiercely and he wore it long, clubbed into a neat queue at his neck. The sun had done its work on his skin, spattering him with a thick covering of freckles and drawing fine lines around his eyes. His beard, so thick and bushy that it almost hid his mouth, had been bleached by the sun to a light, almost coppery, shade. There was a glint of gold at one ear, and Callum was amazed to see that his uncle sported an earring, a gold hoop, so thick and wide that it resembled a wedding ring, something Callum had never seen on a man before.

"Well, have you no words of greeting?" A note of impatience had crept into MacBean's voice.

Callum realized that his uncle was returning his own close scrutiny. He had a feeling of being weighed, so Callum stood as tall as he could and forced himself to speak, although his throat seemed to have closed up and the words struggled to free themselves. "Uncle, I'm pleased to meet you." Behind him, he sensed the innkeeper shifting impatiently. Callum guessed that the man was dissatisfied that his words had yet to provoke a response. "My mother spoke often of you, of your childhood together in the Highlands."

"Aye, we had some happy times." MacBean's face stiffened, his mouth becoming set, the corners turned down. "Your father at least had the courtesy to write me when she became ill and died, and for that I wish I had thanked him. Little but ill will ever passed between him and our family, and now it is too late to change that."

Callum felt his shoulders tense and his voice, when he answered, was defiant. "He wasnae always an easy man, sir, but he never spoke ill of you."

MacBean was silent, staring down at his boots until Callum saw him take a deep breath. "A son should stand up for his father." He raised his eyes, which fixed once again on the innkeeper. "Eli, rather than standing listening to us, why don't you take yourself inside and pour some ale for myself and young Callum here."

With a grunt and clatter of boots, Eli did as he was bid.

Rory MacBean watched until he had vanished into the cool interior before turning once more to Callum. "He likes to mind everyone's business as well as his own, and he's not averse to stirring up trouble but, deep down, he is no a bad man." MacBean looked at the dog, who returned his gaze steadily, and Callum noticed that it was his uncle who looked away first and started to speak — "Eli said this dog" — but then seemed to think better of it, shivering slightly. He attempted a laugh, but it died away. "Someone's thinking about me. Come, let's drink our ale. I want to be home before dark, and your aunt and the weans will be waiting on us.

You and I have much to speak of, and once we're on our way, we'll be safe from providing Eli with more tittle-tattle to spread around."

> ➤ ➤ ➤

Later, when it was time to leave, Callum watched in amazement as the dog, without any instruction, jumped into the bed of the wagon, turned round several times before finding a place to her liking, and then settled her head on her paws, seeming to fall asleep almost immediately. Callum absently fingered the small box, still safely stowed inside his shirt.

Rory clicked his tongue and lifted the reins, and the two oxen ponderously moved off. Their pace was slow, giving Callum plenty of time to stare wide-eyed as they passed a mill and a farm. He wanted to ask questions, but his uncle stared straight ahead and whistled, a mournful tune that Callum remembered his mother singing when she had thought herself alone.

Trees crowded the road on either side with, what seemed to Callum, impenetrable walls. Suddenly, with just a click of his tongue and a light tug on the reins, Rory guided the oxen into an almost hidden break in the trees. Now they were on a track obviously worn by the oxen's feet, and here it was that Rory MacBean finally spoke. "So, a nephew and a dog in one fell swoop! I'll admit that my curiosity has been eating at me, particularly since I've guessed this must have something to do with Eli's little gibe, but I'll no give him the satisfaction of rising to it." His deep voice was gentle, but his eyes never left Callum's face as he waited for an answer.

Callum felt his face burn. "Uncle." His voice sounded hoarse. "I dinna know what happened." He paused, looked back at the sleeping dog and tried again. "There was this man ... and I tripped ... the dog ... he began beating it." Before he could stop them, tears started to run down Callum's reddened cheeks. He turned his gaze and shamefacedly tried to dash the tears away with his hands, but they kept coming. "He offered me the dog and I didnae want to buy it, but something made me." Callum's body shook with the effort of holding in the sobs that threatened to burst out, but words came forth instead, running together in Callum's haste to unburden himself. "I used the money that Dr. Lennie gave me to bring out to you." Hunching his shoulders to take the blow that he expected, Callum whispered, "It was two gold sovereigns."

Rory remained absolutely still.

Callum covered his face with his hands and finally allowed the sobs to come.

"Ah, whisht your noise, boy." Rory laid an awkward hand on Callum's shoulder. "I cannae abide a boy crying." He clicked his tongue as the oxen veered from the track. "I'm not going to lie and say that extra money wouldnae have been of use, but your Dr. Lennie gave me no idea what to expect, so I never made any plans. As long as you're willing to pitch in on the farm that's good enough for me." He smiled ruefully. "Sandy, my eldest, is just eight. He tries but he's still a wee lad in many ways, although he would hate me saying that."

Callum's sobs had died down, but the kindness of his uncle's look and his gentle tone made him feel like weeping again. Searching for the right words, he said, "Uncle," but was unable to continue. He tried to push out of his head all the dread he had felt about coming to Upper Canada, about what life on a farm would be, and promised himself that he would do everything he could to be a help. He tried again. "I'll work hard. You'll no regret letting Dr. Lennie persuade you to take me in."

Rory laughed, a loud, ringing laugh that seemed to bounce off the canopy of leaves. "Persuaded me! Is that what you think? You're my kin, Callum. I'm surprised that, as the son of a Highland woman, you don't know how powerful a tie that is." Rory paused, shook his head. "Ach, why should you?" he said bitterly. "Neither the MacBeans nor our mother's clan, the Chattans, ever showed you that. Both were only too glad to see Ailsa married off and no longer a burden to them. And without being harsh, your father was ever quick to take offense from what I hear, so it was no wonder that the usual ties were severed." He patted Callum's shoulder again. "Family falling outs, the worst kind, laddie. I'm thankful I'm far from such things here. But still," he added, "there was never any doubt in my mind that your place was here when the news came of your father's death." His voice softened. "Ailsa was like a mother to me, when our own mother died. I'd no stand by to see her son brought up by strangers."

As Callum listened, he felt a strange peacefulness grow inside him. He wanted to lean against his uncle and rest his head on his shoulder, but held back, not wanting to be thought a weak child.

Twisting his head around, Rory looked at the dog, who appeared to be sleeping soundly, although Callum would have sworn he saw one eye crack open as his uncle's gaze fell upon her. "That dog's a handsome brute for all that it looks a little battered now. In your place, Callum, I'd have probably done the same. If there's one thing I hate, it's seeing an animal be badly treated."

Callum was surprised when he saw his uncle almost subconsciously cross himself. He heard his father's voice sneer inside his head, "The trappings of Popery!" He wondered whether he would be expected to pray and genuflect, although it seemed unlikely — from what his mother had said, Rory had been an irreligious scamp as a boy, forever tormenting the priest.

Rory continued, "For a dog, that's a powerful presence, and some would say that it's downright uncanny, the way it looks at you. I ..." His voice trailed away as if he had forgotten what he was about to say. He looked at the dog again. "Let's hope it can earn its keep by guarding the chickens against the wild beasties."

Callum let his uncle's words wash over him. He was vaguely aware that his uncle was talking about the farm and his family, but the oxen's steady plodding was making him drowsy. It was only when he sensed the dog stirring behind him and a cold, wet nose pressed itself against his neck that he sat upright and realized that the trees were starting to thin out as they came to a clearing.

Rory's voice had dropped to almost a whisper, and Callum forced himself to pay close attention to what his uncle was saying. "Say nothing about how you came by this dog, do you hear?"

Callum nodded.

"We'll tell your aunt that the dog was a stray who attached itself to you while you waited for me at the inn. She's forever teasing me about being soft-hearted where animals are concerned, so she'll no see anything strange in me letting you keep it." Rory ran a hand over his forehead. "As to the money, we'll tell her there was but a few coppers left over after your fare was paid." He sighed. "Ever since Dr. Lennie's letter first came, you'd think we were coming into a fortune to hear her talk. She's spent that money a hundred times over."

Shrill voices could be heard in the distance, and Callum saw three little figures running toward them. At the far side of the clearing he saw a low building and, in its doorway, a tall woman balancing a baby on one hip.

"Dadda, Dadda!" A small, slight girl, her ginger hair flying out behind her, was the first to reach the wagon.

Callum watched as Rory stopped the wagon and leaped down to pick the girl up in his arms and swing her round. He was unsure what to do, but after a few seconds, he jumped down and stood beside his uncle.

"Ali, do I gather you've missed your old father? I've been gone but the day!" Rory had turned so that the girl was able to peep over his shoulder at Callum. "Do ye see who I found waiting at the inn? It's your cousin, Callum, come all the way from Scotland to be a big brother to you."

By now, the other two children had arrived and were staring at Callum. The eldest, a sturdy boy whom Callum guessed to be Sandy, was red-faced and cross-looking. "If Dougal hadnae fallen and tripped me up, I'd have been here first, not Alison. I'm the fastest runner."

Rory sighed. "It doesnae matter, Sandy. You're all here now and can greet Callum."

Before anyone could say anything more, there was a gentle wuff from the bed of the wagon. The dog was standing up, her head over the side, mouth slightly open and tail wagging.

Alison wriggled out of her father's arms and ran to the side of the wagon, her fingers outstretched, ready to stroke. "A dog! Dadda, did you fetch it for us?"

Rory did not have a chance to reply before the dog jumped down and took up a position alongside Callum, her flank resting against Callum's leg. "There's your answer, my wee flower. This is Callum's dog." Rory looked over the children's heads and winked at Callum. "Decided your cousin looked like a kindly sort and picked him for a master." When Alison's eyes filled with tears, he added, "It seems like a good-natured beast, so I'm sure it'll let you pet it. Isn't that so, Callum?"

"Aye," was all Callum could say, though he had no idea whether his uncle's pronouncement was true. He bent down and patted the dog's head. "Bess," he said, then stopped. The name that the dog's former owner had used stuck in his throat like a fish bone. "That name doesnae suit you, girl. Maybe, I'll just call you Dog until I can think of something better." Aware that his cousins were staring at him, mouths open, he hastily continued. "Dog, these are my cousins, so you be good to them."

The dog made a small noise deep in her throat and slowly padded toward the children, touching each in turn with her nose. She allowed each child to stroke her, lowering her head so that even the littlest one, a thin, wispy boy of about three, could reach.

"Well, I'll be damned!" Rory exclaimed and laughed, putting a hand over his mouth. "None of you heard that, you hear. Your mother would have my skin for using such language, but I never saw the like before. Callum, this dog is a wonder!"

"What's a wonder?" The voice was sharp and accented in a way unfamiliar to Callum's ears. The woman from the doorway had crossed the clearing and was looking at the scene in front of her with a mixture of puzzlement and exasperation.

Rory put an arm around Callum's shoulders and moved him gently forward. "Trude," he said, "here's Callum, Ailsa's son. I found him waiting at Eli's inn, just come from York."

Callum watched the expression change on his aunt's face. Her irritation faded, replaced by a shy smile. He smiled in return, liking the way she brushed her hair out of her eyes with the back of one hand. He remembered his mother making just such a gesture when she was baking. He took off his hat and bowed low, ignoring the snort of laughter that escaped from Sandy. "I'm pleased to meet you, ma'am." He straightened up. "My uncle wrote of you in his letters to my mother. She often said that she wished the two of you could have met."

"La! Such manners." His aunt sighed, and when she spoke again, her voice was wistful. "I've not heard the like, Rory, since I was a girl back near Albany."

Rory MacBean laughed and made a mock lunge for his wife. "Are you saying I've no manners, woman? I may not be a staid old Dutch burgher like your father, but I'll have you know I was schooled with the Laird's son himself before I came to America. Latin, French and some Greek I have, but they do me little good when it comes to clearing a field of stumps. But if it's manners you want, I can still make a leg with the best of them." He started to bow exaggeratedly, pointing his toes and making sweeping gestures with his arms so low that they threatened to raise clouds of dust. Alison and Dougal started to imitate their father — only Sandy stood aloof — and soon their mother was helpless with laughter, the baby in her arms chortling, too. The game ended when Dougal, dizzy with delight, careened into the dog who sat patiently by Callum's side.

Callum reacted quickly, grabbing the scruff of Dog's neck, convinced she would bite the child. He could see that a similar thought was in his aunt's mind, as her smile was replaced by a look of fear. Beneath his fingers, Callum felt no tensing of muscles and he gradually released his grip. Dog gently butted Dougal with her nose as he lay there, still laughing, unaware of the danger he had been in.

"Nice doggie!" Dougal wrapped both his arms around Dog's neck, using her solidity to haul himself to his feet.

Rory, out of breath from his mad gyrations, looked sideways at his wife. "I never did answer your question, Trude, as to what was the wonder, but this is it." He smiled at Callum and winked. "Young Callum, for all of his being a city boy, has the MacBean way with animals. This fine animal knew it and claimed him as her master while he waited for me at Eli's inn." There was a hint of a challenge in his voice when he continued. "I've said that he may keep her. She'll be useful as a guard dog, and you can see how gentle she is with the little weans."

Callum looked from his uncle to his aunt. His heart beat faster and he found that he was sweating. He was acutely aware of Dog, who, disentangling herself from Dougal's grasp, leaned against Callum's leg. Her mouth hung open and she panted gently.

"Oh, Rory, we don't need a dog, particularly not such a great big beast."

Callum couldn't speak. In his head there was a roaring sound, but it didn't drown out the words he wanted to say. *If you don't let the dog stay, then I'll not stay either. I'll take my chances in the forest with the wild animals and the Indians.*

Dog whined and Callum's aunt looked down at her. For a few seconds, they gazed into each other's eyes. Trude shook herself. "Oh, what's it matter?" She laughed. "If we don't keep this dog, I'll wager that you'll come trailing home with another within the month, Rory MacBean. Ever since we lost Jackie to the bear, I know you've been wanting another dog."

Bear! Callum's mouth felt dry. The stories he'd heard in Scotland were true.

"Trude, you're frightening the boy. He's gone white as milk." Rory's voice was gentle as he watched Callum. Gesturing toward the cabin, he said, "Callum's probably exhausted. He's been traveling for weeks, without a decent meal for all that time by the looks of him. The last thing he needs is stories like that." He sighed. "We don't know that it was a bear. Jackie just disappeared."

Sandy interrupted. "But, Dadda, there were tracks."

"Enough, Sandy. You help me unhitch the oxen." Rory's blue eyes stared at Sandy, willing him to remain silent. "Callum, take your box and go with your aunt to the cabin. You can bunk in with Sandy until we get things settled."

Sandy's protest was stifled by another glare from his father. He turned and busied himself with the oxen, his shoulders tense and hunched.

Hefting his box on his shoulder, Callum prepared to follow his aunt. His progress was slow as he had to concentrate on avoiding his small cousins, who, in their efforts to stay close and stare at him, were constantly underfoot. He tried to make sense of everything that had happened, but his thoughts were a confusing blur. The talk of a bear had scared him, yet for the first time in many months, he no longer felt alone. The kindness of his aunt and uncle seemed real. Maybe this place could be home despite it being different from anything he had ever known. He was suddenly aware of Dog walking patiently at his side, and his unease returned. Why had he bought her so recklessly? Why did he feel so attached to her that he was prepared to risk his own future in order to protect her? He shivered and realized that his aunt was talking to him, describing how she and Rory had come here two years ago, leaving the farm her father had established near Fort Niagara. He found her words hard to follow, and it was a relief when they reached the cabin and she pulled a leather string to release the latch of the door. She hurried inside, calling over her shoulder that the baby was asleep and that she wanted to put him in his cradle.

"Callum, Callum, let me show you where you'll sleep." Alison had grabbed his hand and was pulling him over the threshold.

It took a few seconds for Callum's eyes to adjust to the cabin's dimness after the bright sunshine. The scents of dried herbs and wood smoke tickled his nose, causing him to sneeze. He stood in a large rectangular room. A fireplace of stone was in the middle of the far wall. In one corner, half hidden by a curtain, he could make out a bed. His aunt was gently tucking the baby in a cradle jammed between the bed and the wall. At the bed's foot was a smaller bed.

Following the direction of his glance, Alison said, "That's where Mumma and Dadda sleep. Dougal and me too."

Callum looked round. Standing a little in front of the fireplace was a large, roughly fashioned table. Ranged around it were tree stumps that obviously served as chairs. A settle stood on one side of the hearth. On the other side was a battered wooden chest, which Callum recognized as being identical to one his mother had treasured. Above it were shelves holding a few pots, pans and plates and two tattered books. Shivering, Callum twined his fingers in Dog's fur. His home in Edinburgh had not been grand — a minister's stipend made sure of that — but everything here was so primitive. His aunt and uncle had hardly any proper furniture.

Unaware of Callum's dismay, Alison prattled on, pointing to a ladder in one corner. "You and Sandy sleep up in the loft. Mumma made a new straw tick when she heard you were coming. Said that a city boy would be soft and need his creature comforts."

"Alison!" Trude rejoined them and looked down at her daughter's solemn face. "Callum, I can't deny I said that, but I didn't mean it the way young Alison makes it sound. I know what it's like when you're used to better things." She sighed and looked round the cabin. "My father's family had been farming in Albany for nearly sixty years. He was even planning to build a brick house, and then the war broke out and we lost it all."

A thin, grizzling cry came from the cradle.

"Oh no!" Trude's face crinkled in dismay. "Wee Jamie's teething. I can't get him to settle." She went to the chest and got a shawl. "I'll have to strap him to my hip. It's the only thing that seems to quiet him, and at least I have my hands free to work." She looked around distractedly. "Alison, take Dougal and go pull me some carrots, then tell your father and Sandy that dinner will be ready in about an hour." She turned to Callum. "I'll wager you're hungry, Callum, and that dog of yours looks half starved." She waved a hand at the fireplace. "I've a rabbit stew that will feed us all."

The baby's cries rose to a high-pitched wail that pierced Callum's ears.

"I'll have to go to him. We'll get no peace otherwise. Maybe he'll nurse." Trude started toward the cradle, still talking. "Leave your box by the door, then clean yourself up a bit." With that she drew the curtain around the bed, leaving Callum unsure what to do.

A splash of cold water on his face would be refreshing, Callum thought. He scanned the cabin, looking for an ewer and bowl, but could not see any.

Dog buffeted his legs with her head.

"What?" Callum looked at her.

She walked to the door and stopped in front of a wooden bucket of water.

Callum laughed, shaking his head in amazement. "You're a canny beast, all right. It seems you read minds as well as understand what's said."

Dog wuffed and lay down.

Callum squatted by the bucket and began to wash his hands and face, realizing just how grimy he was. He was wishing that he had thought to unpack his box and retrieve the sliver of soap he'd carried on his journey when the door flew open and Sandy stood on the threshold.

"Mumma! Callum's only washing himself in the drinking water." Sandy's tone could not hide his satisfaction.

Callum sprang to his feet, reddening, as he tried to stutter out an apology. "I'm sorry. I didnae know. I didnae want to bother you."

Trude stuck her head around the curtain. "It's all right, Callum. Sandy, don't make such a fuss. Empty the pail, then fetch fresh water from the creek. Take Callum with you so he can wash there."

Callum reached for his box. "If you'll just wait, I'll get my soap."

His words were of no avail. Sandy was already flouncing out the door, water slopping from the bucket. Callum had no choice but to run after his cousin, Dog close at his heels.

Sandy did not look to see if Callum was behind him, but set off as fast as he could around the back of the cabin, seeming to disappear into a wall of trees.

Callum's spirits fell. He didn't understand why his cousin was behaving as he was. He stared at the trees and the darkness under them. Dog ran past him, stopped, looked back, barked and then made for the trees. Unless he wanted to return to the cabin and tell his aunt what had happened — guaranteed to annoy Sandy further — he had no choice but to follow. He set off at a run and soon caught up with Dog, who led him down a narrow path winding between the trees.

Dog ran fast, with strong, powerful strides, and Callum had to run at full tilt to keep up with her. Every so often she let loose a stream of barks. The first time, Callum stopped, and looked fearfully around, convinced that she was warning him of an attack by some beast. But when he saw nothing, he realized she was barking from sheer exhilaration at being able to run so freely. As he pushed to catch her up, he wondered about her former master that such a simple thing could apparently give her so much pleasure.

Mulling on this, Callum did not see Dog come to an abrupt stop, and he nearly cannoned into her, averting the collision only by falling down. As he picked himself up, he heard laughter and there was Sandy standing on the bank of a stream that wound its way through the trees.

"You're a proper gowk!"

Sandy's words, echoing those of Mrs. Lennie, stung, and Callum was torn between giving into the tears that he could feel or shoving his cousin, who appeared to be going out of his way to be unpleasant. A rough, warm tongue licked his hand and he looked down to find Dog panting up at him, her mouth stretched in what looked very much like a grin. Callum couldn't help it. He laughed as well. "Aye, I suppose I am that."

Sandy looked at him in astonishment.

It was obvious to Callum that this was not the reaction his cousin had expected. "I'll not be surprised if I make you laugh a few more times in the coming days. Everything is new to me and I dare say I'll need a lot of help from you not to make a complete idiot of myself." Callum forced himself to smile. "This is the creek, I presume, so I suppose it is all right if I wash myself in it?"

Sandy nodded and watched in fascination as Callum quickly shed his clothes and ran to the water. Dog ran beside him and they hit the water in unison.

The water was icy. Callum rose to the surface quickly and swam vigorously in an attempt to beat the chill. He was conscious of Sandy's gaze fixed upon him. Swimming back to the shallows, he rubbed at the grime of his journey with his hands and then sat on a flat rock where the sun was able to break through the thick mat of branches. He was scanning the water for Dog and was so amazed to see her black head bobbing near the other shore that he had to ask Sandy to repeat the question he had asked as he threw himself down beside Callum, the bucket abandoned. "Who taught you to swim like that?" Sandy was struggling to hide his admiration for such prowess.

Still watching Dog closely, Callum barely managed to reply, "Oh, my father."

"I canna swim, nor can Dadda." Sandy's voice was wistful. Concentrating very hard on not looking at Callum, he finally blurted out, "Would you teach me?"

"Yes, if your father agrees." Callum turned from his cousin in panic and sprang to his feet.

Dog had emerged from the water on the other shore and was standing at the tree line, staring at Callum and Sandy.

"No!" The volume of Callum's shout surprised him. When Dog made no sign of returning, he started for the water. "Dog! Get back here, now!" He hesitated as a thought struck him, turned and ran for his clothes, fumbling at them with clumsy, impatient fingers until he found the box. He clutched this to his chest and shouted once more. "Dog, come here!"

With only the barest of hesitation, Dog turned toward the stream. For a brief moment, she was silhouetted by the sun, and her thick pelt glowed with a nimbus of fire. She turned her head to the trees and howled, a plaintive noise that rose in volume, until all the woods seemed to echo with it.

As she entered the water, Dog's movements were slow. She swam wearily across the stream. At the water's edge, she stood, head down, tail drooping. Callum walked over to her, patted her head. She leaned her head into his hand and then, with no warning, shook herself violently, showering Callum with water, leaving him gasping.

"Gowk!" Sandy said between giggles. "You should have seen that coming. Everyone knows that a dog always shakes itself when it's wet."

Relief that Dog had returned warred with anger, until Callum caught sight of his reflection in the still water of the stream, realizing that his lanky limbs, now mottled blue with cold and spattered with water, deserved Sandy's laughter. He ran for his clothes, dragging them on with some difficulty, trying, without success, to suppress his own laughter. Finally, he gave in and rolled on the ground, great whoops and guffaws coming out of him until his sides hurt and his eyes ran with tears.

Chapter Three

On Callum and Sandy's return to the cabin, everyone was moving so fast that Callum felt useless and in the way. Alison was laying out wooden bowls and spoons on the table. His aunt was crouched awkwardly in front of the hearth, stirring the stew, with the baby strapped to her hip still grizzling. Uncle Rory was maneuvering another tree stump to the table, hampered in his efforts by Dougal, who kept trying to climb onto it.

"Callum, come sit yourself down." Rory's smile was huge and he waved an expansive arm toward the table.

It was the smile that nearly broke him. Not since his mother died had anyone smiled at Callum like that: a smile full of warmth, all the more precious since his uncle hardly knew him. For a second or two, Callum relished the feeling that he had come home and had found a family. Then he felt disloyal to be so easily swayed by a smile and remembered his father laughing scornfully at his mother's quickness to laughter and to tears, saying that such behavior indicated a lightness of mind, and that it was obvious that the MacBeans let their passions rule them. Callum's mother often cried when he spoke like that, which always enraged him more. He would stand over her, lecturing her on the iniquities of her family, how little attention they had paid to her, and how her mother's family was no better, leaving Scotland for England and not even trying to help him secure a better living to support her. Callum had hated his father talking like that; his mother had always seemed so small and frail then. Later, when his father had locked himself into his study, she would try to smile, but the smile wavered, and she told Callum of how things had been different when she and his father had first met. "He wasn't always like this, Callum, believe me. When he was younger, oh, he was so handsome, and yet he courted me, a dowdy old maid, living on sufferance with relatives, trying to earn my keep by acting as governess to their children." She shook her head. "Your father worked so hard to get where he is now; he had such ambitions. Disappointment is corrosive, Callum. It eats away at a man's heart."

Shaking his head to dislodge such unpleasant memories and the feeling of confusion that swamped him as he looked at Rory, Callum said, "Can I help, Uncle?" As soon as the offer was made, Callum regretted it. Everyone seemed so practiced in what they were doing that he was sure he would make a fool of himself yet again.

"No, Callum." It was his aunt who spoke. "There'll be time enough for that tomorrow." She laughed as she straightened up. "I'll warrant that there will be times you'll wish you never made such an offer. The work on a farm is never ending."

Guilty red stained Callum's cheeks, and he avoided his aunt's eyes, which seemed to have penetrated his thoughts so cleverly. "Dog," he said suddenly, happy to divert attention from himself. "May she have some food also? Her last master did not feed her well."

Dog whimpered, and when Callum looked down at her, he was surprised to see drool dripping from her mouth.

"By the look on that poor beast's face, you have a gift for understatement. She's a rack of bones covered in fur." Trude sat back on her haunches, absentmindedly stroking the baby's soft head where it lay against her side. "Callum, there's an old chipped bowl on the shelf behind you. Fetch it down and bring it here. She can eat from that."

Callum did as he was told, conscious of how eagerly Dog followed him to the fireplace.

As his aunt ladled out the rich stew, Callum watched Dog. Her eyes were fixed upon the movements of the spoon between the pot and the bowl, and she whined softly, but, to his surprise, she did not rush forward once the bowl was placed upon the floor. Instead, she lay as close to it as she could get without actually touching it, her muzzle slightly lifted as she sniffed at the rising steam.

"Eat," he said, the irritation rising in his voice as he feared that Dog's behavior might give offense to his aunt. "It's yours."

Dog looked at him, her brown eyes reproachful. Then, with a sigh, she returned to staring intently at the bowl.

Callum jumped as a large hand descended upon his shoulder.

"Let the beastie be, laddie." Rory's voice was gentle. "By', she's uncanny. It's almost as if she knows she'll burn her mouth if she eats it now, however famished she might be. You come and eat, yourself, for I'll wager you have a hunger as powerful as hers." With that he steered Callum to the table and, this time placing both hands upon his shoulders, gently forced him to sit.

After that, Callum was lost in a whirl of senses: the savory taste of the stew as he gulped it down, the rough texture of the bread with which he mopped it up and the noise all around him. Meals at home had been quiet affairs, what little conversation there was delivered in muted voices. Indeed, after his mother's death, his father and he had little to say, and they fell into the habit of reading at table. Here, everyone wanted to talk, often at the same time. At first, he had tried to answer the questions that his aunt and cousins threw at him, but was relieved when Uncle Rory intervened on his behalf.

"The lad's eyes are glazing over. Let him be. We'll have time enough for talk on other evenings." He reached across to his wife and took the baby from her, balancing him on one broad thigh and bouncing him up and down until he chortled and gurgled. "Callum's going to fall asleep with his head in his bowl if we're not careful. Once we've all finished, Sandy, you take him upstairs to the loft while your mammie and I deal with the wee ones and clear up."

By the time Callum followed Sandy up the ladder, his limbs felt so warm and heavy that it was a struggle to force them to move at all. His uncle had to call him three times before he turned back to find Rory holding out his box. With a grunt, Callum took it and passed it up to Sandy, who crouched on the loft floor. As Callum reached the top rung, there was a small commotion below. Sleepily, he turned round. Dog was standing at the bottom of the ladder, her front paws on the fifth rung, whining. Unsure of what to do, Callum made a vague gesture to stay and Dog's whines became louder and more insistent.

"What is the matter with the beast?" Rory had returned to stand at the bottom of the ladder. He stretched out a hand to pull Dog back, but stopped when her whines rose into a plaintive howl. He grinned. "I think you boys have got yourselves a bedfellow. It'll be cramped, but she seems set that where you go, Callum, so goes she." He gave Dog an affectionate slap on the rump. "If you can make it up there, my beauty, you've earned your spot, but there's no one who'll lift you. You're too big a beast for that."

Dog wuffed at Rory. She dropped down on all fours, took several steps back and then took a run at the ladder. Her paws scrabbling for the rungs, she clawed her way to the top, where Callum had to scramble quickly out of her way.

Looking around, Callum saw that his uncle was right; it was going to be a tight fit. A crude platform had been built in one corner of the cabin to form a floor, just big enough to take two straw ticks with a narrow space separating them. Callum stood up and yelped as he banged his head on the ceiling.

Already sitting on his tick and pulling off his boots, Sandy laughed. "Gowk!" he said. With an ease born of long practice, he got off the tick and crouched down, taking a few waddling steps like a duck in the available space.

Callum tried to imitate him, but, hampered by his box and by Dog, he soon gave up and made his way to his bed on his hands and knees, pushing the box in front of him until it hit the wall. He flopped onto the tick, hearing the straw crackle. His eyes closed immediately.

"You cannae sleep in your clothes!" Sandy's voice was incredulous, and he shook Callum roughly.

Callum forced his eyes open.

Sandy had stripped down to his shirt and was staring at Callum with a look of disgust.

Feeling as though he was swimming through treacle, Callum dragged off his jacket and breeches, throwing them into an untidy heap at the foot of his bed. He let himself fall back, his eyes closing before his head hit the pillow, unaware of Dog's soft whining as she inched her way forward so that she could lie with her head resting on Callum's clothes, as close as she could be to the strange carved box.

➤ ➤ ➤

"Callum!" Sandy's voice was a hoarse whisper. When he got no response, he punched Callum's shoulder, none too gently. "Callum, come on. It's time to rise."

Callum sat upright, shaking his head in a vain attempt to regain his senses, which seemed to have lodged deep in a well of sleep. He was confused. Why was Sandy waking him just after he had gone to sleep?

"It's time to get up. Dadda's waiting for us." Sandy did not hide his exasperation. "It's morning, you gowk!"

"But, it's not yet light," Callum complained.

Sandy was already dressed and starting down the ladder. "It soon will be," was his terse reply. "Get your breeches on and come down quietly. We don't want to wake the weans if we can help it. Help Dadda and me with the animals, while Mammie starts on the chores."

"But ..." Callum's objection died on his lips as he heard Sandy descend the ladder. He remained where he was, resentment mingling with tiredness. Sandy had no right to order him around. He had traveled hard and far and, anyway, why did it take three people to look after a few animals? They'd managed without him up until now. It was not as if he'd be much help; more time would be wasted than gained, as they had to instruct him in his new tasks. Callum relaxed at this rationalization and lay down, closing his eyes. Then he remembered Rory's greeting yesterday, and how earnestly he had explained what Callum's help might mean to him and the farm.

A low growl from the foot of the bed caused him to open his eyes again. It was hard to see in the dim light, but he sensed Dog coming to stand alongside him. He could just make her out, a dark, solid blackness that loomed over him. Her head lowered and Callum found himself holding his breath, fearful of the bite that he was certain would come.

Immobile with fear, Callum suddenly felt himself buffeted by her nose as she pushed at him, seeming intent on forcing him to roll over.

"Dog, stop that!" he whispered, mindful of Sandy's warning to be quiet. "What's the matter with you? Leave me be."

Dog pushed him again, harder. When Callum still resisted her efforts, she growled and scrabbled with one large paw at his blanket, pulling it half off him.

His fear replaced with irritation, Callum sat up and pushed her away. "All right, all right! You're in league with Sandy, I can see that. Everyone is determined that I shall not sleep."

Dog sat on her haunches, motionless while Callum struggled in the confined space to pull on his clothes.

Muttering under his breath, Callum felt for the top rung of the ladder and climbed down. At the bottom, he looked up and saw the dark, blocky shape of Dog's head peering down at him.

Ha! he thought. *If you're so keen to be up and about, you can find your own way down. I'll be beggared if I'll lend a hand.* He backed away, bumping into his aunt. As they disentangled themselves, he sensed rather than saw Dog move.

Reaching out with her front paws for the rungs, Dog began her descent. Her momentum seemed to surprise her, and she lost her footing. Callum and his aunt both gasped as she fell, but Dog twisted in the air and, instead of the heavy landing that seemed bound to follow, landed on four paws and made her way to the cabin's door, where she stood patiently waiting.

"You'll find your uncle and Sandy out in the barn." Trude's voice was low, and she turned away before Callum could ask where he might wash or what he might eat.

Callum stumped over to Dog, pushed the door open and stepped outside. The sun was just rising, a glowing orange ball floating above the treetops.

Dog gave a small wuff and ran into the clearing, bounding and leaping. She frolicked for several minutes, even chasing her tail like a puppy.

Callum watched her, sourly at first, but, by the time she came back to his side, panting, and rested her head against his leg, he was unable to suppress a smile. "I may not feel quite like running and leaping, but I'll grant that it is a beautiful sight. At home the sun was hard-pressed to twist its way through the buildings." He sighed. "Come, let's find Uncle Rory and Sandy."

The barn was a crudely fashioned building of logs a short walk from the cabin. A large door in the middle was open, and Callum and Dog peered inside. After the freshness of the early morning light, it took a few seconds before Callum's eyes adjusted. A large pen, for the two oxen Callum had seen the previous day, took up one side. On the other side, there were three smaller stalls. In one, two pigs lay asleep, pink sides smeared with mud. In the second, Sandy crouched milking a cow with an ease that astonished Callum.

Sandy looked up at Callum, his face set and sullen. "You've taken your time. Most of the work's already done."

"Sandy! There's no need to chide Callum." Rory's voice came from the oxen's stall. "He just needs to learn our ways and that'll take a while yet." As he spoke, Rory poured a pail of water he had been carrying into a trough, encouraging the large beasts to drink with a friendly pat on their rumps. He leaned on the side of the stall, smiling at Callum. "Sandy's right. We're nearly done and your aunt will have our porridge on the table soon. Why don't you go and see what eggs the hens have laid for us? It'll give you a chance to look around." Rory climbed up onto the lower rail of the fence and, placing his hands on the top rail, vaulted over, making Dog yip in surprise. Rory pulled a basket off a nail banged into the wall and handed it to Callum.

Conscious still of Sandy's resentful stare, Callum took the basket. Rory's determined kindness plucked at his conscience and he shuffled his feet, unable to meet his uncle's eye. "I'm sorry for my tardiness, Uncle. Show me the henhouse and I'll fetch the eggs for you."

Rory laughed. "I built the wee devils a henhouse, but they rarely stay in it. Look in the undergrowth around the clearing, that's where they like to lay their eggs, never mind that they're easy prey for any passing varmint. Chickens must be the most stupid of all God's creatures."

Dog ran out of the barn. Callum sighed. She seemed to know what she was about, so he followed her. She ran to where the trees started, her nose down as if following a trail. Quivering, she stopped by a large bush and, when Callum was slow in reaching her, let loose a series of small, high yips.

"What? Don't tell me you understood Uncle Rory's instructions so well that you've found a hen for me. This I cannae believe." Shaking his head, Callum bent down and gingerly poked at the leaves closest to the ground.

A flurry of feathers and squawks exploded from the bush. Callum rocked back on his heels and fell over. By the time he recovered himself, the hen was long gone. Dog nudged him and he reached in, his hand closing on the smoothness of an egg, still warm from the hen's body. Callum smiled and gently laid the egg in the basket. Seven more times, Dog led Callum to nests. By the final one, he no longer jumped when the hen flew off.

Fondling Dog's ears, Callum crouched down and looked her right in the eyes. "I've never had a dog so I dinna really know what they're like, but even I can tell that you're a marvel. If you had but hands like me, you'd be far more of a help to Uncle Rory than I ever will be." Dog whimpered and licked Callum's hand. He hardly noticed because he was looking off into the distance, and his voice was low when he spoke again. "It's all so strange that I'm going to need a marvel to help me." Straightening up slowly, he said, "Come on, let's go and show them what we've found."

Callum's welcome at the breakfast table was all he could have hoped for. Rory exclaimed over the number of eggs he had found, declaring that they would make a farmer of him yet. His little cousins regarded him with awe and fought over who would sit by his side. Only Sandy remained aloof, pulling a face when his mother said that maybe egg gathering should always be Callum's job as he, Sandy, did not take as much care and there were always several cracked eggs when he collected them. Callum felt himself glow with all the praise and admiration, falling upon the porridge and milk his aunt served with relish. He was just looking hopefully for a second helping when Rory stood up.

"Right, my lovelies, let us get this day's work started."

Callum was astounded. Surely, the chores were all done. He had half formed a plan to spend the day reading the one book he had brought with him, by the creek, maybe even swimming if it proved warm enough. He watched in astonishment as little Alison stacked the bowls and carried them carefully to the door. Dougal trailed behind her, carrying the spoons. There they waited for their mother, who, with the baby firmly strapped to her hip, led them out of the cabin. He knew that his mother had worked hard to run their little household, but she had always had help in the form of her old nursemaid, Annie MacBean, who'd come to them when Callum was born and stayed, even though all she was offered was her keep. Here, it would appear that there were no servants — work was everyone's lot whatever their age, work that more often than not was physical. Callum shivered, remembering how determined his father had been that he pursue the life of a scholar and never have to work with his hands as his father once had. He was wondering what he would have made of Rory, an educated man who willingly chose such a life.

Just then, Rory's voice cut into Callum's musings. "What say you that we take on the mighty stump? With Callum's help we might defeat that monster yet, eh, Sandy?" Rory rubbed his hands and strode toward the door without waiting for an answer.

Callum would still have been standing still had not Dog bumped him with her nose, and Sandy grabbed his sleeve and tugged until the choice was to fall over or move.

Sandy kept a grip on Callum, leading him out toward the edge of the clearing. "Dadda and I have cleared a whole acre ready for the wheat planting."

Pride was evident in his voice and the way in which he puffed out his sturdy chest. "He said that he couldn't have done it without my help. I mayn't be able to chop the trees yet, but I did the bundling. If we can but move this big stump, then we can do the burning."

Callum looked at his cousin. It seemed to him that he was speaking a foreign language: "bundling" and "burning" — what did this have to do with planting wheat? The sun was fully up and Callum felt sweat trickle down his back. He thought longingly of the creek's cool water.

Rory stood waiting for them, hefting an ax and two tools the likes of which Callum had never seen. "Just this stump and we'll have another acre ready to dry out in the sun. Ah, Callum, I love trees but they're the bane of a farmer's life." He patted Callum's shoulder with his free hand. "Land is what we need, clear land where we can plant our crops." Seeing Callum's uncomprehending look, he added, "When you've been with us awhile, you'll realize that the forest is our adversary. But enough philosophizing. There's work to be done. Callum and Sandy, you dig down, uncover the roots as much as you can, then I'll chop them." He handed Callum and Sandy the two tools. "Callum, you take the mattock and break down the soil on this side. Sandy, you use the hoe as best you can. While you do that, I'll chop the branches we cut yesterday."

Callum lifted the mattock. It felt heavy and awkward in his hands, and when he brought it down beside the stump, it seemed to bounce off the soil, hardly making a mark. He swung it again, harder, and was pleased to see that this time he broke the hard, dry soil. He sensed he was being watched and looked up to find both Dog and Sandy staring intently at him. Callum swung again, and Dog yipped, settling herself down in the shade to watch. Sandy swung his hoe and for several minutes the two boys worked hard. Sweat ran down Callum's face, stinging his eyes, dripping off his nose. He wiped his hand across his forehead, but it did little good. He sneaked a glance at Sandy, who was seemingly unaffected by the heat. Callum threw off his jacket, tossing it near where Dog lay. She moved her head so that it rested upon the jacket. The blade of the mattock met resistance on his next swing and Callum dropped to his knees, scrabbling with his hands to uncover a large, knotty root.

"Leave it. Dadda will cut it. Move on round." Sandy did not slow down at all as he spoke.

Callum marveled that such a small boy should have such endurance and, trying not to pant, did as he was told. The palms of his hands burned but he forced himself to continue. Gradually, he found a rhythm that seemed to help, and soon his whole being was concentrated on the rise and fall of the mattock, the sweat that ran freely on his body and the unfamiliar ache in his shoulders. The dull sound of the ax behind him told him that his uncle was chopping through the roots. A few seconds later, he stiffened. Familiar Gaelic words washed over him as his uncle began to sing in a deep, tuneful baritone. Sandy's thin, high voice joined in, and Callum found himself transported back to the fireside in Edinburgh, sitting on the settle with his mother and singing the very same song with her. He stopped swinging the mattock and roughly wiped his eyes with his shirt sleeve. He started as a warm, rough tongue burred its way up his hand.

Dog had risen now and stood beside him. She butted his leg with her head, and Callum hugged her, grateful for a way to hide how deeply the song affected him.

"She's an affectionate beast to be sure." Rory had stopped work, too. "Well, lads, I think we're ready to try and pull this monster. Sandy, go see whether your mammie needs you for any chores. Callum can help me harness up the oxen." He waited until Sandy was out of earshot and added, "Sandy tries, but he's more of a hindrance when it comes to a job like this. Keenness doesn't make up for lack of strength, and I'm always afraid he'll get hurt, but it's rare that he'll be told."

As Callum and Dog followed Rory to the barn, he thought of how hard it had been after his mother died, how his father had refused to talk of her, how he had had to lock his memories away and how those memories had grown hazy, so that sometimes Callum struggled to recall what she looked like. Here, in this strange land amongst unfamiliar people, the memories were forcing themselves upon him. Little things his uncle did, the songs he sang, his kindness, even the way he tilted his large head to one side when listening to Callum, all these made Callum think of his mother again, leaving him feeling hollowed out and empty.

A sudden commotion forced Callum out of his reveries. The oxen were shifting uneasily in their stall, stamping their hooves and snorting.

"Husha, husha." Rory's voice was low and soothing, but had no effect.

Callum stepped closer to the stall, curious to see what was causing them to behave so. As he did, the nearest ox lurched toward the side of the stall, crashing into it with one huge shoulder.

Callum jumped back. Dog set up a furious barking, which seemed to inflame the ox even further, and it made another bone-jarring lunge at the fence.

"Callum! Get out of here, and take Dog with you." Rory's tone was urgent, brooking no disobedience.

His heart racing with fear, Callum ran outside and flung himself down on the grass. Dog stood beside him, growling softly, the fur on her back standing up. Callum stroked her, murmuring, and she gradually quietened, even though she remained standing and alert by his side.

It was some time before Rory came out of the barn leading the oxen, who followed him placidly until they caught sight of Dog. They both planted their hooves solidly and refused to move no matter how much Rory encouraged them or tugged at their harness. Through clenched teeth, as he strained to move the oxen, Rory hissed, "Callum, it's Dog. I dinna know why, but they've taken against her. Take her away from here. Otherwise we'll never shift them."

Callum got wearily to his feet, puzzled, but willing to do as his uncle wished, only to find that Dog was already going — albeit with her teeth bared in a silent snarl — moving slowly backward so as not to lose sight of the oxen.

"Dog! Enough!" Callum's voice was sharp.

Dog's ears drooped, her shoulders dropped, and, with her tail almost dragging on the ground, she stopped glaring at the oxen, as if she was ashamed to have been caught in such childish taunting. Moving close to Callum's side, she followed him as he made his way back to the cabin, where he found his aunt and the children weeding a large plot of vegetables.

"Callum, has Rory sent you to help as well?" Trude laughed. "At this rate, our little garden will be a picture. I've never had so much help."

Callum shook his head. "Dog has to stay here. We don't want her in the way." Sensing that his aunt was about to object, Callum said, "She'll just lie quietly, won't you, Dog?"

In answer, Dog trotted over to where the baby lay on a blanket in the shade of a berry bush and lay down next to him, resting her head on her paws. A heavy sigh was the only sound she made as Callum ran back to the field where his uncle waited.

In Callum's absence, Rory had wrapped and knotted ropes tightly around the stump and then tethered these to the oxen's harness. Two more ropes remained loose, and it was one of these that Rory handed to Callum. "We'll pull alongside the beasts, for I warrant that this monster will take all the strength we can muster."

At the click of Rory's tongue, the oxen started to move ponderously forward, and all Callum had to do was keep pace with them, holding his rope loosely. He glanced over to his uncle and saw that Rory was holding the rope over his shoulder and had secured the end around his waist. Callum scrambled to do likewise. The rope tautened and, to avoid being pulled back, he leaned forward, feeling the rope bite through his thin shirt. He envied his uncle the coat of thick unbleached cotton he was wearing. Everything seemed to slow down, seconds stretching like taffy. The oxen strained in place, their hooves taking tiny mincing steps. It took all of Callum's strength to stay upright when the great stump resisted their efforts to pull it free.

Just when Callum's vision began to blur with black spots dancing in front of his eyes, Rory grunted, "Drop the rope, Callum." He let his own rope drop and clicked at the oxen. His face was as red as his hair, with sweat streaming down. "I felt it give, but there's something still holding it. Grab your mattock and we'll see if we can clear it."

Callum's legs and arms were loose and shaky, but he obeyed, feebly raising the mattock and bringing it down under Rory's direction.

"There's our culprit!" Rory's voice was triumphant as he pointed to a thick, twisted root that disappeared into the ground close to the trunk. With several powerful blows of the ax, he cut through it. "Come on, lad. We'll do it this time."

Wearily, Callum got into position and started forward with the oxen, every muscle pulled to breaking point. He could hear his uncle panting as he urged them on. A ripping sound came from behind him, and Callum toppled forward as the stump finally came free of the soil like a rotten tooth pulled from a gum. He fell to his knees and stayed there, sucking air.

"Come on, Callum. Don't lollygag. We've only just started. I know it's hard at first, but you'll get used to it. Go fetch Sandy. You and he can dig up as many of the roots as you can."

Once Sandy was back, Callum's world narrowed to a haze of digging, pulling and chopping. His back ached, and the burning in his hands had become an inferno. A fat blister formed by his thumb and burst, leaving a raw patch that stung constantly. He wanted to shout, "Enough!" but was shamed into silence by the solid way Sandy kept working. He continually reminded himself that he should be grateful, that his aunt and uncle were giving him a home, but his physical woes drowned these thoughts out, and all he could think about was what a leisurely way he had spent his time at home in Edinburgh, reading or studying under his father's guidance.

When the sun was high in the sky, and when Callum thought he would die unless he could stop, Rory finally called a halt. In his mute desperation, Callum had not noticed Alison arrive, struggling under the weight of a basket. "Lunch is here, laddies," Rory said. "We'll eat, then we'll burn off the field."

Every single part of Callum's body hurt, and he could not find a comfortable way to sit when he flung himself down in the shade beside Dog, who had accompanied Alison. He fell upon the bread and cheese as if he was starving. No food had ever tasted so good, and it was gone much too soon.

"Hard work gives you an appetite, all right." Rory smiled as he looked at Callum. "I'll wager that you never did this back at home." He laughed. "Mind you, it wasn't what I had in mind for myself either. When I was your age, my head was stuffed with dreams of fine chevaliers, but as the youngest son of an old father, there was little for me at home. My stepbrothers made sure of that." Rory looked quizzically at Callum. "Did your mammie tell you about how they were grown men with families of their own by the time I was born?" When Callum nodded, Rory continued, "When my father died, America with my uncle was my best bet, and a comfortable living it would have been, too, but for the war." Rory's smile became rueful. "At least here I'm my own master, and we must make the best of what we have."

Callum knew that what Rory said was right. What choice did he have? He had never felt so tired in all his born days. Shutting his eyes, he lay back, letting his uncle's voice wash over him, talking of how the Highlanders had settled the Mohawk Valley, how big and rich the farms were, how his family farm had been lost and how Rory's uncle had died in battle, leaving Rory, only a few months older than Callum was now, to fend for himself. If it hadn't been for the kindness of two older men, one Dutch, one English, Rory did not know what might have become of him. It was obviously a familiar tale because every so often Sandy or Alison would finish their father's sentences, yelling with delight at the mention of the Dutchman. "That's our Opa!" Alison poked Callum in the ribs and, sure that she had his attention, helpfully added, "Our mammie's dadda."

Callum managed a smile, but soon found his mind drifting. The coolness of an Edinburgh autumn replaced the hot Canadian sun. He and his mother sat on a grassy bank beside the castle. She sewed and sang while he read a book of poems, marveling at the writer's skill, longing to be able to write so beautifully.

The memory was shattered by Sandy pulling roughly on Callum's arm. "Dadda asked you a question!" He sounded indignant.

Callum shook him off, none too gently, and sat up, all too aware of the heat and how uncomfortably his shirt stuck to his body.

His voice mild, Rory said, "Don't fuss, Sandy. Callum was miles away. All I asked, laddie, was what you wanted to be." He had started to add, "Mebbe a minister like —" when Callum burst out, "Not a farmer!"

There were a few seconds of silence.

Sandy's mouth hung open in a perfect O.

Callum could not believe what he had just said, but a small, secret part of him rejoiced.

A frown creased Rory's forehead. "There's honesty for you." His mouth twisted as he fought back a smile. "Me neither," he added with a giggle that made Callum see the mischievous boy he had once been, the boy whom Callum's mother had loved so dearly. "But," he said, shaking his head, "that's what I am and for now, Callum, I'm afraid that's what you are, too."

"Aye, I know." Callum knew that he sounded sullen and did not mean to do so. He tried to smile but the smile did not seem to want to stay in place. When he got to his feet, his limbs felt heavy and awkward. The only comfort he could take was in the solid presence of Dog by his side.

She remained there all afternoon, keeping out of his way, but close enough that he could ruffle the thick fur on her neck. While Rory manhandled the chunks of chopped stump away, Sandy directed Callum in breaking small branches and brush, spreading them as evenly as they could upon the cleared ground. When it was done, Rory dismissed the two boys.

"I'll set this alight and watch it burn. We've cleared enough so that it should not spread. There's time that we can let it lie in the sun for weeks before planting." He walked over to where Callum and Sandy stood, placed a hand on one of each boy's shoulders and looked solemnly at them. "You've worked well, boys. For that you have my thanks."

Callum felt a glow of pleasure at the praise, but it vanished when his uncle added, "I let the pigs and cow loose this morning to forage. Sandy, show Callum where they'll likely be and then bring them back and set them up for the night."

Sandy set off running, leaving Callum amazed at his energy. Wearily, he followed, Dog at his heels. As he stumbled along, Callum kept up a muttering. "Is there never any time alone in this place? For all his kind words, Uncle Rory is a hard taskmaster."

Sandy had disappeared into the trees and, although Callum could hear him, he could not see him. "I'll be beggared if I call out to him," he said. "If I take my time, perhaps I can rest a few moments here. He's sure to come back this way once he's got the beasts." There was a hollow at the bottom of a tree and Callum settled himself down to wait.

Dog stood still in front of Callum, looking first at him and then toward the sound of Sandy's crashing progress. She whined, then whirled and ran into the forest, barking as she went, a sound that seemed to Callum to resonate with a joy he couldn't understand.

Callum started up with a cry of "Dog!" but she had already disappeared. He looked nervously around. The bright sunlight in which he had worked all day did not penetrate the thick canopy of trees, and he found himself in a place of shadows and half light. Whereas he had prepared himself to relish the silence, now it seemed sinister. He remembered his aunt talking about a dog called Jackie and a bear. A noise behind him made him spin round, but all he saw was a flutter of leaves as something small moved by. Heart racing, Callum ran, praying that he was going in the right direction. Branches and leaves whipped in his face, but he did not care. All that mattered was that he found Dog. He felt for the box and stopped when he realized it was in the pocket of his jacket, which lay abandoned where they had worked. Panic set him running faster until a root snagged his foot and he went tumbling. When his fall stopped, a now-familiar rough tongue raked his cheek. Dog stood over him, her lips pulled back as if laughing at his predicament.

"She's faster than you, that's for sure." Sandy stood close by. The pigs were behind him, rooting at the base of a tree. "And she's more use. One look at her and the cow took off for the cabin as if the hounds of hell were after her." He giggled. "Pigs are none too keen on her either, but when they find acorns, eating comes first." He walked over to where Callum lay and stretched out a hand.

Callum took it and struggled to his feet, brushing off his clothes. He moved so that he stood as close to Dog as he was able, watching Sandy as he herded the pigs by making little runs at them, until he got them headed out of the forest.

By the time the pigs and cow were in their stalls, the light had taken on the thinner glow of late afternoon. Callum had retrieved his jacket and taken out the box, placing it inside his shirt. Every so often he found his fingers tracing its outline where it lay against his skin. Callum found every step and movement an effort. He struggled to follow Sandy's instructions. Even dashing water half-heartedly over his face and hands from a bowl his aunt had left by the cabin door for them was a huge effort.

Inside the cabin, there was the hustle and bustle of the previous night. The two little children were amusing the baby by bobbing an acorn on a string in front of his face as he lay in his cradle, so that he chortled and squeaked with joy. Rory was carving a joint of meat while Trude stirred a pot at the hearth.

"Callum and Sandy, bring me the plates," Rory called, "then sit yourselves down. I'll wager that you two will eat well tonight."

Rory's prophecy was proved true. Callum could not remember ever having felt so hungry. He hacked at the meat that Rory served him, eager to get it into his mouth, but irritated by the way he was forced to stop chewing to answer the questions about his life in Edinburgh that his aunt and Alison seemed so excited to ask. As the meal drew to a close, a drowsiness crept over Callum, and he struggled to keep his eyes open and his head from falling forward onto his chest. Sandy tugged on his sleeve and indicated that he should help clear the table, a chore Callum stumbled through. When it was done, Alison took Callum's hand and led him to the hearth, where Rory had pulled some of the tree stumps from the table alongside the settle.

"On most nights, Dadda reads to us," she said, and then, with a huge grin, she added, "or tells us stories about the wee folk. Do you know any stories about them? I love those stories."

Callum almost smiled down at Alison as he remembered his mother regaling him with tales of kelpies and boggarts that she had brought with her from the Highlands, tales she dared tell only when his father was out visiting parishioners. How he too had loved the stories, but he had always felt guilty listening so avidly to them. "Arrant nonsense!" his father would thunder. "Logic and reason, that's what you should build your world upon, Callum." Callum sighed, logic and reason hadn't enabled his father to provide for his son, and it had been no help to Callum in convincing Dr. Lennie to let him stay in Scotland.

"No," he said abruptly, irritation flooding through him. "I don't. I'm tired." He looked round for Dog and gestured with his head to the ladder leading to the loft.

Without a sound she got up from the hearth and loped over to his side.

Once in the loft, Callum stripped off his shirt and breeches and lay them with his jacket at the foot of the bed. He had been sure that sleep would come immediately, but it did not. He could hear the bass rumble of Rory's voice, the children's soft laughter. His eyes felt hot and itchy. Soon tears ran down his cheeks. He turned onto his side and faced the wall.

Dog whined and moved so that she lay alongside his back, a warm presence.

When Sandy came up, Callum pretended he was asleep, although tears still flowed and it would be many hours before sleep finally came.

Chapter Four

Days passed in a blur for Callum. Always tired, his body was racked by unfamiliar aches as he tackled the never-ending chores that he realized were the lot of everyone save the baby, Jamie.

The routine never varied: up at first light, tend to the animals, return to the cabin for breakfast, then whatever Uncle Rory decreed as the main work of the day, lunch brought to them as they worked, return the animals to their stalls for the night. The days he hated most were those they spent clearing land of trees and brush. Although his hands had quickly toughened up, so that he handled the mattock with ease, the monotony of digging and chopping bore heavily upon Callum.

Not even the Sabbath brought any respite. On his first Sunday, Callum was roused at dawn as usual. They fed and watered the animals before breakfast and, as Rory rose from the table at the end of breakfast, Callum could contain himself no longer.

"Do you not go to church today?" he blurted out, his voice louder than he intended.

Rory smiled at him. "I'll wager, Callum, that you spent most of Sunday in your father's kirk, would that be right?"

"Aye," Callum said. Rory's tone was light and teasing, but, somehow, Callum felt Rory disapproved. "It was a day for quiet contemplation."

"Ah, now that would be lovely. Quiet contemplation, indeed." Rory gestured expansively at the family still seated round the table, waved a hand toward the open cabin door. "But with this lot here, and the animals, there's not much time for that now, is there, Callum, as you've come to know."

"Yes, Uncle, I see that, but don't you go to town to worship?" Callum's thoughts lightened at the possibility of a break in routine.

"What for, laddie? There's no church built yet, although I know some of the families have plans to do just that." Sensing Callum's disappointment, Rory continued, "Even if there was, we're such a mixed package, me Catholic and Trude Lutheran, there'd be no place that would suit us all. No, Callum, a man doesnae need a church to worship. He can make his peace with God alone, by being part of His great creation." Rory stood up. "Come on, lads, we've got work to do."

Callum was frozen to his chair, shocked to his very marrow that the Sabbath would not be observed, and by the ease with which Rory dismissed the fact that Trude was not a Catholic. Why had she not converted upon her marriage? It had not been a problem with his own parents, as his mother's family, the Chattans, had long since left the Catholic church for the Presbyterian one, and Ailsa, a poor relation in their house, had done so, too, eager to fit in and be accepted. Still, Callum just knew that his father would not have even considered marriage if Ailsa had stuck to the Catholic ways of the Highlands. Callum's musings were abruptly disturbed when Sandy sidled up and whispered in his ear, "Dadda's teasing you. We'll work this morning for sure, but Sunday afternoons are times for frolics and fun. You'll see."

Even an afternoon when he was able to spend time alone, save for Dog, did not cheer Callum up, and the monotony of daily life began to tell upon him. At times he thought he would go mad. Only Dog's constant presence made it bearable. She rarely left his side, Uncle Rory sending her away only if they were working closely with the oxen. Callum found peace in her company, her small barks and the look in her soft brown eyes that offered encouragement and comfort. On occasions, when he was sent to work by himself, she even provided guidance, leading him to the spot Rory had directed when Callum had stood daydreaming. It was at these times that Callum talked to her, pouring out his troubles, both real and imagined.

"Ah, Dog, I cannae bear much more of this. I work like a beast. They all do in this New World." He held out his hands to her. "Look at these. These are the hands of a working man, not a scholar. I swear that my fingers are so thick and clumsy they'll not hold a pen, let alone write a fine hand." He picked up the basket in which he was meant to be collecting blackberries. "And as for my studies, my father would weep to see how they are neglected. All I have is the book I brought with me, and I must know it frontward and backward, so many times have I read and reread it. Uncle Rory may well be an educated man but he seems to allot little time for studies."

Dog looked up at Callum and whined.

"What's the matter?" He laughed. "I think you're contradicting me, aren't you, you canny beast? To be sure, we do spend the time after dinner reading, and Uncle is teaching Sandy his numbers and Alison her letters. And, I know, I know that if he didn't concentrate his energies on the farm, we'd all starve in this wild land. But man doesnae live by bread alone ..." His voice trailed off and he smiled wistfully. "Do you know, Dog, one of the books he has is in French? It's by the great philosopher Voltaire. I'd dearly love to know French. Uncle has said he'll teach me, and I know he means to, but I don't see that he'll ever have the time."

The unremitting heat also troubled Callum greatly. The clothes he had brought with him were heavy and unsuited to the work he now did.

After repairing yet another rip in his linen shirt, Callum's aunt had shaken her head. "I know you have one other shirt, Callum, but that will be in tatters, too. Rory has an old hunting frock that I was saving for Sandy, but it will do you in the meantime."

Callum was about to protest. A frock was surely something that a girl would wear. The picture it conjured, of big Rory simpering in muslin, made Callum laugh out loud, and when he explained his confusion to Trude, she joined in. "Ah, now that would be a wonderful sight indeed, but I forget, Callum, how different things must be for you here." She rummaged around in the chest near their bed and pulled out a coat made of rough unbleached cotton, with two short capelike attachments to its shoulders. "Here it is. This is a hunting frock. Try it on."

Callum did as he was bid and was surprised to find that the coat did not swamp him as he had expected. It came a little below his knees, whereas it would have been mid-thigh on his uncle. The biggest surprise was in the shoulders. His uncle was so broad and muscled that Callum thought the frock would have hung from his much thinner frame.

Trude bustled round him, pulling the material to make it fit. Noticing Callum's expression, she said, "Ya, you've filled out, young Callum, since you've been with us. Hard work will do that to you. Was your father a tall man?"

Callum nodded. In his dark clerical suit, his father had always reminded him of a huge black-feathered bird.

"When you finish your growth then, I'll wager you'll be a big man, too." Trude patted him on the shoulder. "This will not take long to fix. Then you'll be more comfortable."

Trude's words proved true. Callum had thought the hunting frock would only make him hotter, but somehow it did not. Although he continued to sweat as he had never done before in his life, he was at least protected from the brambles and branches that were a part of daily life.

Callum only ceased to sweat at night, and then not every night, as the air in the sleeping loft hung heavily upon him. He was aware of a sour, vinegary odor that hung about his body, and he bathed in the creek whenever he could. There was always an hour between the end of the day's chores and supper being served, and Callum would take off as fast as he could. If he dallied, Sandy was sure to follow. Callum knew he had promised to teach Sandy to swim, but the time alone was such a precious thing. Once at the creek, he'd strip off his clothes and leap into the cool water. Dog seemed to love swimming as much as he did and she swam powerfully up and down, but never deigned to retrieve the sticks Callum threw for her.

Nearly a month after his arrival, Callum could not resist trying again. "Come on, Dog. Fetch!" When she did not move, or even acknowledge that she had heard him, Callum shook his head. "You're a strange beast. I thought all dogs liked this game."

Dog stood still at the water's edge and looked reproachfully at Callum. She scraped the wet earth with one paw, her claws leaving three straight lines. She was repeating the action, drawing three more lines, this time horizontally across the first, when Sandy burst through the brush and ran up to her, his pounding feet smashing through the design she had made.

"There you are!" he exclaimed. "I've been looking all over for you." He was panting slightly. "Dadda said that you were probably here, so I came." Sandy smiled a shy, hopeful smile. When Callum said nothing, he added, "Dinner's not nearly ready yet."

Dog was standing on the bank, her shoulders drooping, her plume of a tail hanging low and dejected. Suddenly, she shook herself, barked once and then ran into the water, splashing Sandy. She stopped, looked back at him and barked again. Then she turned and stared at Callum.

Callum couldn't help himself. Despite his resentment at being discovered, he laughed. Sandy looked so hopeful and even Dog's jaws hung open, which Callum had learned to recognize as an expression of happiness. "Mistress Dog seems to have decided that it is time I made good on my promise to you, Sandy, so get yourself ready for your first swimming lesson."

Sandy's smile broadened, and he hastily shed his clothes and took a few tentative steps into the water. "What do I do, Cousin?"

Callum's face became serious. "All I can do, Sandy, is show you what my father did when he taught me to swim." He beckoned Sandy to come closer, crouched down and said, "Put your hands on my shoulders, and let your legs float up onto the water's surface." Seeing his cousin's worried look, he said, "If you'll but believe the water will support you, it will. Come, try it. I promise I'll not let you sink." There was a catch in Callum's voice as he remembered his father saying the very same words.

They'd gone on a visit to the small fishing village where his father had grown up. Callum's mother had stayed in Edinburgh, still weak from the effects of a summer cold that was reluctant to leave her. The sun was hot, unusually so, as they walked along the beach littered with drying nets. Callum's father had shaken his head ruefully at the nets, talked of how hard he had studied to avoid becoming a fisherman like his father and his brothers, how hard Callum was going to have to work in order to find a place for himself in the world. Then, without warning, he had said, "Let's swim!" a rare smile on his face. They had spent the afternoon in the waves, by the end of which time Callum could swim. It was one of the only occasions that Callum remembered his father laughing out loud. A precious memory, indeed.

Sandy's hands gripped Callum's shoulders so tightly that he was sure he would have their imprint for days to come. His eyes were tight shut, and his face was screwed up as if he was waiting for a blow to fall.

"Sandy, it's not that bad. You're the one who's been crazing me to teach you this!" Callum searched his mind for a way to calm his cousin's fears. "Imagine that the water is your bed and that you are lying upon it."

Sandy opened his eyes and Callum detected a slight lessening of tension, but he knew that if he let Sandy go, he would sink, spluttering and fighting the water.

He was at a loss when Dog swam up and nudged him with her nose. "Not now, Dog," he said, "I'm busy."

Dog would not be dismissed, and she continued butting Callum with her head until finally he paid her some attention. She swam alongside Sandy as close as she could get to him and remained there, treading water, looking meaningfully at Callum. He stared back at her and then exclaimed, "Ah, Sandy, Dog is offering to pull you, I think. Put your arms around her neck and kick your legs. You'll see that you can do it."

Sandy was reluctant to let go of Callum's shoulders, even though the water was still shallow enough for him to stand, but he was eventually persuaded to do as Callum suggested. With his arms clasped around Dog's thick neck, his body supported by her broad back, Sandy finally relaxed and, although his grip tightened as she started to swim, he was soon laughing and kicking for all he was worth. As his confidence grew, Sandy loosened his grip and even floated on his own. Dog yipped encouragingly as Callum showed Sandy how to use his arms as well as his legs to propel himself through the water.

Sandy was so pleased with his new-found skill that he started to jump and splash, shrieking with laughter. Both Callum and Dog joined in and it was thus that Rory found them when he came down the path.

"Boys!" Rory had to shout to make himself heard. "Your dinner's been on the table for a considerable time."

Responding to the volume of Rory's voice rather than its gentle tone, Callum hung his head.

"What's kept you so long?" Rory stripped off his own shirt and used it to roughly towel down Sandy, who stood shivering beside him. "Look at you, you're both all over with goose pimples. Get yourselves dressed quickly. Some rabbit stew will soon sort you out."

"Dadda! Callum's taught me to swim." Sandy's eyes shone and he made a dart toward the water again. "Let me show you!" he shouted, before Rory caught him and steered him back to his clothes.

"Another time, laddie." Rory turned to Callum. "Is this true?"

Callum was struggling to force his wet limbs into his clothes. A small flame of jealousy stirred in him as he watched Rory hug Sandy to him, his pride evident despite the brusqueness of his voice. "Aye. He followed me here. I didnae ask him to come. Anyway, it wasn't really me. Dog was the one who showed him that there was nothing to fear in the water."

Rory threw his arm around Callum's shoulders, almost knocking him off balance. "It was a kind act, Callum." He lowered his voice, so that only Callum could hear. "Don't think that I don't know how much you value your time alone. We all have precious little of that."

Callum pulled away from his uncle's embrace and bent down to stroke Dog, anxious to hide how hard his uncle's words struck home. Just as he did so, she shook herself and, once again, Callum found himself splattered with water.

Sandy started to laugh. "You've not learnt, have you? Gowk!"

Laughing, Callum took off running, not waiting for the others but comforted by the fact that they and Dog were close behind.

After that, Sandy followed Callum most days down to the creek to swim. Callum would have dearly loved to find another place where he could have the solitude he craved, but the one time he tried, Dog planted herself in front of him, growling softly. So he stayed, resentful but resigned that Dog had decided he was to watch over his small cousin, who loved to leap and frolic in the water like a puppy. A routine developed. Callum would swim, then, after drying himself and dressing, would sit reading on the bank. Dog often stayed in the water with Sandy, and Callum was surprised at how jealous this made him feel. On rare occasions, when no other chores claimed him, Rory would join them, and he made good his promise to start teaching Callum the rudiments of French.

It was only a little while before Alison and Dougal began to feel that they were missing something, and they begged and pleaded to go down to the creek as well. At first, Trude had protested, saying they could go only when Rory was there, but Dougal cried so much and Alison was such a nuisance that she was forced to reconsider, despite her fears that they were too young to be so far from the cabin without their parents. Rory had considered the matter gravely and then had said, "Callum's shown himself responsible enough with Sandy. He'll no doubt do the same for the two wee ones." He had given Trude his most beguiling smile. "And I'd like them to swim, too, not be an old stone like their Dadda, who'd sink right down to the bottom!" He fell to the floor and lay there, his mouth opening and closing like a fish's.

Trude had laughed and flapped her apron at Rory. "Ach! Rory MacBean, you could charm the bees into giving you honey. All right, we'll see, but, Callum, you must be sure not to let them wander, especially Dougal, who can never resist exploring."

Callum had solemnly promised, quietly proud that Rory had such faith in him. Indeed, the guardianship was not onerous once he had taught each of them how to swim. He felt safe leaving them in the water while he retired to his favorite spot under the trees. If any of the children attempted to move beyond their depth, Dog was there, firmly steering them back to safety, either with gentle buffets from her nose or by offering a broad back to cling to while she towed them in.

There came a day though, when Callum was jolted out of his complacency.

The weather had been hot all week, and by the Saturday everyone was short-tempered and the children were fractious. Alison seemed to take delight in tormenting Sandy; she had a knack for finding the words or even a look that would quickly reduce him to fury. Rory, normally the most gentle of fathers, had threatened them both with a good hiding — Alison for her wicked teasing, and Sandy for hitting his sister in rage. Neither paid him much heed and continued their niggling. Finally, Rory broke and yelled, "Enough! Callum, take them to the creek, duck them under until they become friends again!" Both Alison and Sandy giggled at this and it restored their good humor at least until they got to the creek. With squeals of delight, Alison and Sandy shed their clothes and ran into the water, followed closely by Dog. Dougal, who had not yet mastered the art of buttons, stood and watched them.

"Cannae I help you, wee one?" Callum asked, bending down.

Dougal shook his head, his thick blond hair swinging. "Nah!" he said, with great certainty. "I'll watch today."

Callum smiled. His little cousin was a law unto himself, with moods and fancies that were difficult to predict. "I'll stay on the bank with you and read then," he said. "If you should chance to change your mind, we can go in together later." Callum watched Dougal until he found a stick and some stones and started arranging them in patterns in the dirt. Taking off his boots and stockings, Callum settled down with his back against the trunk of his favorite tree and read.

For a few minutes, all was peaceful, until Sandy and Alison fell out once again. Alison had perfected a way of swimming that, whenever she passed close to Sandy, became outrageously splashy. He, naturally, retaliated and, within seconds, they were screaming and splashing. When they both lost their tempers, they wrestled in the water and made such a commotion that both Dog and Callum bounded toward them. Although Sandy outweighed Alison considerably, she wrapped her wiry legs around Sandy's waist and had fistfuls of his hair locked in a death grip. He was howling in pain, and even as Callum prized Alison's reluctant fingers free, the two still struggled to have at each other. It took Callum at least five minutes before the two sullen children stood still. Dog circled them, whining uneasily.

"By all that's holy, what is the matter with you two? I've never seen the like before." Callum finally had the two antagonists apart. "Dog!" he called. "Come here. Stand in front of Alison." Callum squatted, facing his cousins. Both Sandy and Alison looked shamefaced, hanging their heads and reluctant to meet Callum's gaze. "Your dadda would be ashamed of you both. Alison, you're being deliberately provoking, and Sandy, you're older, you should ignore what she's doing and not respond." Callum realized that Alison was not listening to him, but was gazing toward the bank. He gently tried to turn her head to give him her full attention, but she resisted and almost whispered, "Dougal's gone, Callum."

A sick feeling raced through Callum as he scanned the trees round the creek for some sign of his small cousin. Seeing nothing, he quickly herded Alison to the bank, motioning Sandy to follow. "Stay here and get your breeks on. Dog, stay with them. I'll go search for the wee devil." Callum tried to make his voice sound calm, almost amused by Dougal's mischievousness, but he knew that he was doing a poor job of disguising his terror. He received no argument from Sandy and Alison, whose eyes were huge with wonder and fear.

Without glancing back, Callum set off down the path, alert for any clue as to where Dougal might have gone. He couldn't have strayed far, for he only had little legs and the argument had but distracted Callum for moments. A sound to his left caused him to pause, and when he peered through the underbrush, he could see a clearing and, in it, a flash of white that could only be Dougal's shirt. His heart slowed down from its panic-fuelled pounding, and he forced his way through until he got to the clearing. Dougal, his mouth smeared red, sat cross-legged in the center. He was holding his shirt out from his body to form a pouch that still contained a few wild raspberries. Snuffling and grunting came from a small bear cub as it buried its snout in the pouch. Dougal was laughing with delight and crooning, "Nice beary, nice beary!" just as he might have spoken to Dog.

Callum's first reaction was to snatch the boy into his arms, but he forced himself to remain still. No harm was being done, and the bear seemed a small, harmless thing, not at all like the fearsome creatures that had so haunted his dreams of the Canadas. He wondered what it would be like to touch such an animal. Its fur was a peculiar shade of black, almost rusty looking, but it shone and looked thick and soft. He started to move cautiously forward, trying not to startle either Dougal or his new friend. A soft noise behind him halted his progress. Turning round, he saw that Dog had disobeyed him and was surveying the scene in the clearing with her deep brown eyes wide. As Callum raised a warning finger to his lips, the bear cub lifted its head and noticed both Callum and Dog.

"Hanh!" it grunted, and jumped back from Dougal in such a comical way, as if each of its paws had springs attached, that Callum could not help laughing. For a few seconds, it remained absolutely still, all its attention focused on Dog. With as small a gesture as he could, Callum tried to signal to her that she should move back, but she would not move, and started to growl softly.

"Whisht your noise, Dog. You're frightening it. Can you not see that it's just a babby?" Callum was fascinated by this creature. How wonderful it would be to tame it and bring it home. Now *that* would be a story to tell.

Dog's growling was becoming louder, and she moved forward. The bear cub skittered back, farther from Dougal, and then froze as if unsure what to do.

Callum was about to scold Dog when he realized that a piece of shadow on the far side of the clearing was moving. A coughing grunt came as it emerged into the light. Callum took a step back. A large bear, dark and looming, reared up to its full height. *This must be its mother*, Callum thought. Despite his racing heart, he felt strangely calm. Time had slowed and he saw the minutest details: Dougal's small fingers quivering as he let his shirt fall, the tiny hairs on the raspberries as they tumbled to the ground, a strand of creeper that clung to one of the bear's ears, giving it a rakish air. Without making any conscious decision, he found himself moving forward, leaning down and scooping Dougal into his arms.

The cub whined in alarm, but seemed unable to move. The mother grunted again and dropped down on all fours, her small eyes locked now on Callum, cradling Dougal against his chest. She ran, a run that surprised Callum with its speed. He tightened his grip on Dougal, determined that when the bear bowled them over, he would not drop him. He shut his eyes, muttering a prayer and bracing himself for the impact.

It never came.

"Hunnf!" the bear snorted, and Callum could smell its breath, rank and sweet. He opened his eyes. The bear stood calmly, but a short distance away, its cub by its side. Dog sat in front of Callum, her tail wagging very slightly. Her head was tilted to one side, and she let loose with a series of growls and yips. The bear seemed to be listening to her. It shook its head, then whiffled and grunted back in turn. This strange dialogue went on for several minutes. Thankful for his cousin's safety, Callum held Dougal tight, savoring the solidity of the small body that could so easily have ended up bloody and broken. Dougal, completely unaware, wriggled in Callum's arms and clapped his hands. "They be talking!" he crowed as if this was the most natural thing in the world.

Up close, Callum could see how terrifyingly huge the bear was, towering over Dog. She had broad shoulders, and her paws ended in sharp talons. As she grunted, Callum caught glimpses of powerful brown-stained teeth. The fear that had been strangely absent during the whole encounter now hit him hard. Dog, as if sensing something, glanced back at him. Then she got very deliberately to her feet, moved toward the bear, touched her nose to its nose and whined softly. The bear made no noise in reply, but reached out with one huge shovel-like paw. A cry rose in Callum's throat but lodged there, as, with surprising delicacy, the bear lightly cuffed

Dog's shoulder before ambling away into the forest, her cub a miniature shadow at her side.

Callum stared at Dog, who stood as if she had been turned into a statue by the bear's touch. He called her name softly and, when she didn't respond, knelt by her side. Her eyes were fixed on the place where the bears had vanished into the undergrowth. Two silver trails of tears slid down her face. Callum shivered despite the heat.

"Ah, I wish you could talk, bonny lass." Callum's voice was rough. "Tell me what that was all about."

"She can," a small voice whispered. "She talked to the bear." Dougal was tugging Callum's hair in an attempt to get his attention.

Without thinking, Callum said, "There wasnae a bear, Dougal. It was all a dream."

Dog finally moved. She turned and gravely regarded the two boys, until her gaze locked on Dougal. She stared at him intensely, and Callum was amazed to see his small cousin's eyelids become heavy and then close. His breathing deepened, and he let out a small snore. Dog came and sat by Callum, leaning heavily against his leg. Every so often she stared into the woods and whined.

A crashing through the undergrowth announced the arrival of Sandy and Alison, who had grown tired of waiting by the creek.

"You found him!" Alison's voice was joyful and she ran and hugged Callum's legs. Sandy was less demonstrative, his arms laden with Callum's book, stockings and boots, but he smiled at his brother.

"Aye, he decided to go berry hunting!" Callum looked down at where Dougal had dropped the berries in fright. "If we look around, I'm sure we'll find some more to take back with us."

Dougal stirred in his arms and woke up, seeming amazed to find himself away from the creek. He started to speak, then stopped, looking puzzled. "Berries," he said, "raspberries."

Callum looked down at Dog. She gave a small bark.

➤   ➤   ➤

That night, the treat of the raspberries was much praised. Callum pleaded tiredness in order to go to his bed early. He lay on his tick, one hand stroking Dog's broad back, thinking about what he had seen, of how close they had come to disaster. Through such melancholy thoughts, Dougal's words, "They be talking," kept circling in his head. His mother had told him how the Sith, the fairies of the Highlands, could understand the language of all birds and animals, and how they sometimes gave a mortal that power, too. He wondered what Dog might say to him if he had been given such a gift. Callum fell asleep still puzzling over the enigma that was Dog, determined to unlock her mystery.

Such thoughts faded quickly the next day, when the usual round of chores began. Callum did not even notice that Dog was more restless than usual and strayed to the edge of the wood whenever she could, whining when Callum called her back. He was in a black mood. Rory had taken barrels of ash to sell in the village and to pick up supplies. Callum had hoped that he might go along, for he had met no one but Eli and his uncle's family since his arrival. But his hopes came to nothing when Trude said that Callum's help would be needed to prepare their harvest of corn for winter storage.

"Wee Jamie's teeth seem to be bothering him mightily." She looked apologetically at Callum. "I know this is woman's work, but the baby's so grizzly that I'll not get anything done, and we can't leave the cobs outside much longer. Raccoons have already been at them."

Disappointment must have shown on Callum's face, for Rory's voice had been gentle when he spoke. "Another time, Callum laddie, you can come with me and see our little community. I'll teach you how to deal with the storekeeper, for he's a wily old trader who'll skin you if you're not wise to him."

Callum shrugged. He tried to keep his face expressionless. "What do I have to do?" he asked his aunt, keeping his eyes down, fighting back the anger that was filling him up.

Sandy laughed. "He doesn't even know —" but he got no farther, for Rory uncharacteristically snapped, "That's enough, Sandy." Turning to Callum, his voice gentle once more, he said, "You've seen two large stones, one on top of the other, in the barn? Well, that's a quern. Your aunt will show you how to use it. I'll be bound that she'll have you grind what remains of last year's corn in it for her today." Placing his hand in the small of Sandy's back, he gently propelled him out of the cabin. "You, young man, can profitably spend your day weeding the vegetables and then you can gather reeds from the creek as we need to make more baskets."

For Callum, this day was the longest he had yet spent. Aunt Trude's explanations of what he had to do were drawn out and involved for what seemed to be simple tasks: pulling the husks back and tearing the corn silk off, setting aside the best cobs for seed, scraping kernels off the rest and spreading them to dry. Aunt Trude worked alongside him, stopping often to suckle the baby. Alison and even little Dougal worked, too, and Callum's resentment grew ever stronger — why was he needed for tasks that such little children managed with ease? Only when sent to grind the corn into meal did his anger abate slightly. The two stones took all his strength to lift, and his arms soon ached from turning them as Alison poured kernels into the top of the quern. The grinding itself was monotonous, and Callum could find no comfortable position. If he sat, he did not have enough purchase to push the heavy stones around. Kneeling worked best, but his back and arms soon ached, and sweat made the wooden turning handle slick and hard to hold. By lunchtime Alison and Dougal's whining mirrored exactly how Callum felt. Only Sandy was in a good humor, his wet hair indicating that gathering reeds had turned into a sneaked swim. Callum glared at him.

Callum felt as if he had been ground between the rough stones of the quern. In an attempt to cheer up the children, his aunt had set out lunch for all of them in the shade at the edge of the clearing, bringing them some precious maple sugar, but it did little good. Sandy and Alison had resumed the niggling of each other that they were so good at. Dougal was in a huff, although would not say what it was about. Even Jamie was howling. Trude sat down on the grass with a thump, half-heartedly rocking him. Her face was white and strained. Callum noticed that she made no move to eat.

Callum felt a twinge of guilt and reached out. "Let me take him while you eat." The baby was rigid with the effort of shrieking, his small face red and sweaty. Holding him gingerly, Callum placed him against his chest so that Jamie could see over his shoulder to where Dog lay in the shade. It was magical, the crying stopped instantly. Awkwardly, Callum jiggled Jamie up and down and Jamie responded by chortling. He lifted him away and looked into his face. "See, wee Jamie, life's not so bad, is it? Not when you've got food to eat, a big cousin to play with, and a mammie who loves you!" His words had been spoken without thought, but Callum shivered.

When peace had settled on the group and his aunt had taken her lunch, Callum handed Jamie back to her. As he did so, she reached up and stroked Callum's cheek. "You have a gentle touch, Callum, although I think you would try to hide it."

Callum did not trust himself to speak, so he gathered up food and went and sat as far as he could from the others. He ate his food quickly and then lay down, turning on his side so that he faced Dog, who had followed him and now sat panting in the shade.

"Ah, Dog, you have it easy. No mindless chores for you," he said, sighing. "Would that I were you. Then I might be happy, not realizing in what captivity I am held."

Dog whined, but Callum did not heed her.

Tired from his morning's exertions, he drifted into an uneasy and restless sleep in which his limbs twitched and once he shouted out. So he remained until Alison came to tell him that it was time to return to work. As he stood up, he looked strangely at Dog, who met his gaze unflinchingly. Shaking his head as if to clear it, Callum spoke. "I had the strangest dream, Dog. At first, I thought I was you, running through the woods, but then, although I was a dog, I knew I was a person. I was running as fast as I could because I knew that if I did not, I would lose the thing most precious to me in all the world. Even as I ran, I knew I was too late, but I still had to try." Callum shivered. "I felt so alone. What do you make of that, Dog? Are my brains finally addled by this hot Canadian sun?"

Still staring at Callum, Dog barked, not her usual full-throated bark but a small, forlorn one.

The strange dream troubled Callum the rest of the afternoon, especially as every time he looked up from his work, Dog was staring at him, more fixedly than usual. Several times he shuddered, and it was with relief that he joined the hubbub that greeted Rory's return, just as his chore was close to completed.

Rory smiled as everyone ran toward the wagon when it entered the clearing. He leaped down and snatched Alison into his arms and whirled around until she begged him to stop. Dougal squealed for the same treatment, and it was only after this had been done and Rory had caught his breath and regained his balance that the reason for his smile was revealed.

"We are to have an outing!" he announced grandly.

"All of us?" Sandy asked, hopping from foot to foot, his fingers pressed to his mouth as if he could scarcely believe such good news.

"All of us," Rory confirmed. "Major Nicholson's man was at the store. He was riding to all the homesteads to ask for labor for the harvest in three days' time. I saved him the trip here and signed myself and Callum up. The pay's good and we'll just pray that the weather holds so that our own harvest can be delayed. The women and children are to serve as gleaners."

Callum must have looked puzzled for Alison piped up, "We'll scour the field for dropped grains once you've harvested and stooked the wheat."

One part of Callum seethed at the fact that his uncle treated him like a servant whose labor could be sold without even asking him, but joy surged at the thought that finally the workaday routine would be broken and that he would see and have the company of others.

"And then ..." Rory drew his words out teasingly. "And then, Major Nicholson is providing a harvest supper for all. Eli will bring his fiddle and we shall dance the night away." He grasped Trude's hand, put his other hand in the small of her back and danced her around the wagon. Their laughter rang out and even the baby joined in, forgetting the pain of his teeth while being jounced around in such a novel manner.

Callum smiled and did not resist when Alison, a miniature of her mother, held up her arms to him. He picked her up and danced her round.

Chapter Five

On the day of the harvest, Callum, for once, didn't mind leaving his bed even before the sun had fully risen. A mist, gray like cobwebs, covered everything and muffled the sounds as the family readied themselves for the off, but it could not dampen the excitement that fizzed inside everyone. All chores were carried out quickly. The wicked blades of the two sickles, which Rory carefully wrapped in sacking and stowed in the wagon bed, caused Callum but a moment's dismay that he was expected to handle such dangerous things.

Rory helped Trude and the baby up onto the wagon's seat and then turned to find that Sandy was already in the wagon, receiving the two smaller children, whom Callum was lifting up. He laughed. "Such eagerness I rarely see. Jump up, Callum, and we'll be on our way."

Callum did as he was told and then was nearly knocked over as Dog leaped into the wagon.

"Maybe Dog should stay here." Trude had turned to Callum. "Major Nicholson keeps a pack of hounds ..." Her voice trailed off as she saw the anger surge in Callum's face, twisting his mouth into a snarl.

His words, when he finally gained enough control to speak, were spat out. "If you'll not let her come then I shan't come either."

"Callum, Callum, you have no cause to speak to your aunt so!" Rory's tone was steely, the look in his eyes unyielding. "An apology is needed if either you or Dog is to come."

Callum hung his head, unable to look at his uncle. "I'm sorry," he muttered. "I ..."

"Hardly gracious, but it will do." Rory looked long and hard at Callum. "I know how much the beast means to you, but she is no more than a beast. It will be your charge to see that she behaves at all times, and that you work as you are expected to do." He sighed. "We need what money we can earn today to buy more livestock."

Callum said nothing. He sat in a corner of the wagon bed, shocked at his own rage and how close he had come to forfeiting the outing. Dog whimpered, and he put his arm around her neck, burying his face in her coarse fur. He remained so, ignoring the whispering of his cousins, until the wagon emerged from the forest and they started down the rough road that led to Coote's Paradise.

Callum recognized the mill he had seen on the day of his arrival and then Eli's inn, but beyond that, everything was new to him. The road — although Callum found it hard to dignify it with such a title — was straight if deeply rutted, and he became aware that trails led off into the trees that grew thickly on either side.

"Please, Uncle?" Callum's curiosity overcame his fear of displeasing Rory further. "Who made this road and where does it go?"

"It's the Governor's Road, made by the military. It runs all the way to the border." To Callum's surprise, Rory sounded his normal, affable self as he turned and smiled. "If those American rebels give us any more trouble, then troops can be moved quickly along it. As for maintaining it, everyone whose land touches it is expected to make sure that their frontage is clear of regrowth." He laughed. "That's another job for you and me, boy, when the colder weather comes."

Callum subsided into silence, thinking about his uncle's words. "American rebels" and "troops" sounded wild and worrying. Yet one more thing that made this place so alien.

A shout from his uncle brought him out of his reverie. Another wagon, as loaded as their own, was on the road a little ahead of them, and, if Callum strained his eyes, he could see several more. Callum was eager to see what these people were like, but before his wish was granted, he saw something amazing. The trees had gradually thinned out and he saw, on either side of the road, broad, well-tended fields. There was a turning off the road that led to a large house that sat surrounded by outbuildings on the crest of a small hill. Twelve wagons were either stopped or were making their way toward the house.

"Why, it's a proper farm!" Callum exclaimed, and then flushed as he realized what his words implied.

"Aye, that it is." Rory sounded amused. "So, you see, Callum, there is civilization here, and it's what we all aspire to, although without Major Nicholson's family money, which pays for all he needs, *we* have to work long and hard."

Work! That's all there was here. But his gloom did not last long and, once they had found a spot to stop that met with Rory's approval, Callum was able to look around, noting how weatherbeaten all the men looked. He looked down at his own hands and saw that they too were a deep brown.

His aunt and uncle seemed both well known and well liked, for they were greeted heartily by the others. Rory placed his hand on Callum's shoulder and drew him forward, introducing him. Callum felt his resentment at the work to come lessen slightly as he heard Rory's words. "This is Callum Murdoch, my sister's boy, come all the way from Edinburgh to join us here. For all that he is a city boy, born and bred, he learns fast. Since he's come,

I've cleared more ground than ever before." Rory's voice got louder as a man, better dressed than any Callum had seen since his arrival in Canada, picked his way gingerly toward the knot of men. "At this rate, in a couple of years, it'll be me who will be hiring at harvest time."

"Still full of grand ideas, eh, MacBean?" The man's voice was dry, the words clipped.

Rory's grip on Callum's shoulder tightened. "Aye, and there's no law against them, Major Nicholson. Though I'm sure some of your fancy friends in York would like to make it so."

Callum was shocked that his uncle spoke so defiantly, his jaw jutting. He watched Major Nicholson closely, waiting for him to explode and send them packing. Had Uncle Rory lost his senses? Did he not know that one didn't talk to gentry like that, particularly gentry who might grant you preferment? Instead, Major Nicholson smiled — a thin-lipped smile, but a smile all the same.

"Ever the fiery dissenter, MacBean. Your tongue has not lost its edge. Let's hope there's a similar one on your sickle." Nicholson looked around at the assembled men. "You'll need it. It's a record harvest, boys, so let's get to work." Without waiting for a reply, Major Nicholson turned and walked away.

A servant, dressed all in black, came forward and quickly divided the men into groups of three:

two to cut and one to bundle. There was a small commotion as Rory insisted on himself and Callum being matched with an older man whose rangy limbs were corded with sinew. The servant was obviously put out, but the look in Rory's eyes made it clear this was not negotiable. Callum sighed — there was so much that was confusing here, not least the manners.

"Callum, this is Joshua Mason, my oldest friend, the man who led me to this paradise on Earth!" Rory was expansive as he retrieved the sickles from the wagon. "If he and Trude's father had not gathered me up like the stray lambie I was, I doubt I would have survived a battle let alone the war!" He leaned closed to Callum, his eyes dancing with laughter. "Now, if Josh, here, hadnae sired all his sons first before producing a daughter, he could have been my father-in-law!"

Mason laughed. "Nay, Rory, once you set eyes on Trude, and she on you, there was no doubt that you would wed. It quite turned my stomach to see the eyes you made at each other." His gaze fell on Callum. "You've noticed, boy, that your uncle lets nothing get in the way of a good tale. Believe half of what he tells you, and you might be somewhere near the truth."

Callum was unsure what to say, so he contented himself with nodding. He guessed that Mason was the other man whom Rory had mentioned caring for him after his own uncle had died in battle. Callum was left puzzling why the name seemed so familiar and then he remembered. Mason was also the man from whom Rory had collected the barrel on the day of his arrival.

The threesome set off toward the fields. Rory and Mason were deep in conversation. This suited Callum because it gave him time to look around. It was hard not to stare open-mouthed at what he saw. The house was two stories, made of painted clapboard. There was even glass in the windows. Through these, Callum saw fine furniture and, to his amazement, one room that seemed to contain nothing but books. He couldn't help himself. He moved closer, peering in. A boy a little younger than Callum sat at a table, books and paper spread in front of him. An elderly man stood behind him, leaning over and pointing to something on a page. The boy was rolling his eyes, looking anywhere but where the pointing finger indicated. His gaze finally fell on Callum. He stuck out his tongue and then made a dismissive gesture with his hand.

"Arrogant little swine, isn't he?" Rory's words shocked Callum, who had yet to hear him speak ill of anyone. "That's Nicholson's eldest boy," Rory continued, "and his tutor. Some poor relation, I heard." Rory laughed, a bitter laugh that Callum had not heard before. "Still, I'll wager that the 'poor' relation could buy and sell most of us, and as for Nicholson himself ..."

Mason joined in, his voice deep and measured. "Aye, well, there's those that say that Nicholson's elder brother, some kind of lord he is in England, will pay anything to keep him out of the country."

Rory spat. "For the rest of us, all we have is our labor, and our health. We'll make ourselves as good a living as Nicholson one of these days." He sighed. "It's hard though, Callum, isn't it, to see that? Don't your fingers just itch to turn the pages of those books? I know mine do." Rory's voice was wistful and he too stared in at the window, defying the look of irritation lodged on the tutor's face.

"Is this boy an educated one like you, MacBean?" Mason's tone was wondering, and Callum felt himself blush under such scrutiny.

"He is that, Joshua. Taught by his father. Fluent in Latin and Greek, and he writes a fine hand."

Callum was conscious of the pride in Rory's tone, and he felt a surge of affection for his uncle, which quickly died as he recalled how little chance he had to use his learning.

Unaware of the feelings that raced in Callum, Rory started walking again, still talking. "Young Callum's a bonny scholar. I've started to teach him what little French I have, and he picks it up so quickly that he'll soon outstrip me." Gesturing back toward the house, Rory said, "A tutor like that is what Callum needs. He'd pay more attention than Nicholson's lout, that's for sure."

Mason snorted. "Precious little hope of that. Before you came, some of us approached Major Nicholson and asked him whether our children could join in lessons."

Rory shook his head. "I'll warrant he gave you short shrift."

Mason chuckled and, imitating Nicholson's clipped tones and precise voice, said, "To what end? Farm boys don't need to study books." Mason's face darkened at the memory. "As far as he's concerned, laboring is all we're fit for. You're all right, Rory, you're an educated man and you can teach your own children if you have a mind to, but there's a lot of us who barely know our letters and figures. How will our children learn?" Anger was building in Mason. "We weren't expecting charity. We mayn't have coin, but we offered payment in kind. The bastard laughed at us. 'I have all that I need,' he said, 'and why make your families do without for something that will only make them dissatisfied.'" Mason's face was set. "That made me all the more determined. We'll find a way, if only to spite Nicholson." He looked hard at Rory, who took a step backward, his hands held up as if to ward Mason off.

"No, you're not thinking that I'm your man. The farm takes all my time." Rory's tone was firm but regretful. "You'll have to look elsewhere.

Why ..." Whatever Rory had been about to say was lost in a fusillade of barks that suddenly issued from Dog, who had been following them unnoticed. She ran forward, still barking, and seemed to scan the field in front of them. At its far side, a man disappeared into the woods.

"Dog! Dog! Calm yourself." Callum knelt beside her. The barking stopped, only to be replaced by low growls that caused her whole sturdy frame to vibrate.

"What's the matter with yon beast?" Mason had moved forward and was looking quizzically down. "Is she vicious?"

Rory shook his head. "No. She's as gentle as they come. Trude even trusts her to play with the weans. She's Callum's dog. Attached herself to him the day he arrived." He crouched beside Callum. "Do you ken what's amiss, boy?"

Callum, his heart beating fast, mumbled a negative reply.

"Keep her under control, Callum." Rory straightened up. "Let's get to work. Josh and I will cut and you can stook, Callum. Watch how we do it, and then you can spell us." Rory stepped forward, and with a few powerful strokes he cut a line into the wheat. Dropping his sickle, he took a handful of wheat stalks and knotted them at one end. He then gathered an armful of wheat and wrapped the first handful of wheat around its middle, knotting it securely. "This is a sheaf, Callum. Tie ten of these and prop them up and you'll have a stook." The whole thing took but seconds, and Rory resumed cutting, joined by Mason.

Callum stood behind them and attempted to tie a sheaf himself. The first part was easy, but he found that the wheat had a mind of its own when he tried to make a bundle of it: the stalks were both slippery and spiky, sliding out of his grasp while pricking his hands. He muttered under his breath and persisted until he had something that resembled the neat bundle Rory had made. He turned to Dog to seek her admiration, only to find that, once again, she was growling softly. He followed her gaze and saw that she had fixed upon a man at the far side of the next field.

Shaking his head at Dog's odd behavior, Callum concentrated on his work and soon fell into a rhythm of bending, tying and propping. He surprised himself when he felt a prick of pride as Joshua Mason complimented him on his work and then showed him how to swing the sickle.

Dog settled down, lying in the shade at the edge of the field, but Callum sensed a restlessness about her, an uneasiness that caused her to get to her feet and to whine and growl, and him to touch the strange carved box that he always carried inside his shirt. As he worked, Callum realized that Dog's attention seemed centered on one of the groups in the farthest field.

The end of the day's work was signaled by the arrival of Nicholson's servants bringing out tables to set up in the fields, followed by the women bearing platters of meat and vegetables. Only when everyone drew near the feast that was being laid out did Callum recognize the object of Dog's intense scrutiny and unease. It was the man who had sold her to him, swaggering in their direction. His stare was focused on Dog, and a smile caused his mouth to twitch.

"Do you know yon fellow, Callum?" Rory was staring hard at the man, his face indicating that he did not like what he saw.

"He's the man who sold me Dog, Uncle. The man who was at Eli's inn."

Mason joined them, carrying three tankards of ale that he had snagged from a passing server. "That fellow's been hanging round the area for the last week or so, got just about everyone's back up. Asks for work, turns nasty if you don't give him any, but he's an idle jackanapes and you get little in return for whatever it is you give him." He snorted and handed two tankards to Rory and Callum before he continued. "Came out to my place when I was in the woods. Young Amy was looking after the little ones and he made her right uneasy with the way he looked at her and the way he wouldn't leave when she told him that I was the one he should see. By the time I came back, she'd taken the children into the cabin and barred the door. He was sitting on a stump by the door, looking like he owned the place." Mason turned to Callum. "Come to think of it, before I drove him off, he was asking questions about a red-haired boy and a dog." Mason laughed. "Not having met you, young Callum, I told him he was wasting his time and that there was no such person for miles around."

The thick fur on Dog's neck and shoulders stood up in a ruff. She took several stiff-legged steps forward, her growling becoming louder as the man stopped a judicious distance away from where she and Callum stood.

Callum's mouth was dry and his heart was racing.

Finally, the man spoke. His smile had broadened but was belied by the tone of his voice, which carried a full load of eager malice. "So, my newly arrived friend and the lovely Bess. I thought I might come across you here. Was our transaction worthwhile? Is she a good doggie?" As the man smiled, the rows of tattooed dots on his cheekbones seemed to writhe like black snakes.

Callum shivered and felt inside his shirt for Dog's box, his fingers tightening on it, causing Dog's growl to falter. She looked up at Callum before turning back to the man, snarling, fangs showing, as he made a move to step closer.

"You always were an ill-tempered bitch!" The words were spat out, puzzling Callum until he realized they were directed at Dog. "Still, that made the mastery of you all the sweeter." The smile grew wheedling as the man returned his attention to Callum. "Young stranger, I don't suppose you would consider selling Bess back to me, would you?" His eyes glittered and he reached down, attempting to grip Dog's ear, snatching his fingers back as she lunged at him, jaws snapping. "I find my days strangely empty without the spice of her company, the enjoyment of her servitude."

Callum's shout of "No!" was almost swallowed by the sound of Dog's frantic barking. Callum was suddenly aware that the busy preparations of the harvest supper had ceased, and everyone was watching him and the man.

Disappointment and anger caused the man's face to contort and flush a dark, sullen red. It was obvious he was struggling for control. When he finally spoke, his voice was determinedly pleasant. "No need to be hasty, young man. I'll make it worth your while."

Calmer now, Callum said, "No, I said no!" His hand reached down and touched Dog's thick fur, the touch bringing back memories of the welts and tangles he had felt the first time he had stroked her.

His voice strengthened by passion, he added, "You were no fit master for her! I'd never let any animal back into your care to be beaten and half starved!"

All pretense of courtesy vanished and the man took a huge stride toward Callum, his arm raised to strike him down where he stood.

Callum was unable to move. He closed his eyes and waited for the blow. It never landed.

A grunt of exhaled air freed Callum from his paralysis. He looked up to see the man immobilized, locked in the delivery of his blow. Rory had come from behind Callum and grasped the descending arm in his powerful grip, forcing it to remain just above Callum's head. Dog had positioned herself in front of Callum. She appeared to be twice her normal size. All her fur was standing on end, and in her gentle brown eyes, there were flickers of fierce yellow as she stared fixedly at the man. A noise, the like of which Callum had never heard, was issuing from her throat. Something like a whine, but one that had within it a repetitive pattern of sound rising and falling like a chant. It increased in volume and intensity until Callum felt the hairs on the back of his neck rise and he wanted to clap his hands over his ears.

The effect on the man was terrifying. His eyes rolled up in their sockets. His lips, flecked with foam and spittle, drew back from his clenched teeth in a strained, silent snarl. His body jerked, and he would have fallen to the ground in a faint had not Rory still held him.

Pushing Callum back with his free arm, Rory lowered the man to the ground, where he lay, limbs still twitching.

"By all that's holy!" Rory stopped, unable to say more.

Dog's weird ululation ceased as abruptly as it had begun. Her fur still on end, she strutted toward the fallen body, sniffed it and then squatted beside it and let flow a copious stream of urine, whose hot, rank stench caused those nearest to turn away.

Callum was trembling. It was all he could do to call Dog to his side. Conscious of everyone's wondering, he prayed that she would come immediately.

Her fur restored to its usual sleek state, Dog strode majestically to where Callum waited, her head held high, ignoring those who stepped back when she passed, pulling their children close. She flopped heavily on the ground beside his feet, resting her head upon her paws, the picture of a quiet animal at rest, but Callum saw that her eyes did not stray from the fallen figure.

No one moved to help the man.

"Good God, MacBean, what was all that? What kind of animal are you harboring?" Major Nicholson's voice rang out and, as if it was a signal, a hubbub of conversation replaced the silence.

Rory's reply was lost in the noise that now surrounded Callum. Whatever it was, it satisfied

Nicholson, for he laughed, and his high tenor voice sliced through all other sounds. "Former owner, you say? A mite too fond of the stick. Your young nephew must have treated the beast kindly to inspire such devotion. What a sight the animal was! Magnificent! If she ever whelps, I'd not say no to one of her litter. Make a grand guard dog." Realizing that people were milling around aimlessly, Nicholson raised his voice further. "There'll be more entertainment later, but the food is spoiling. Let's eat."

People moved toward the tables. Trude and the children had come to stand near Rory, and when Callum went to join them with Dog, he was aware of the furtive looks they were receiving. Fear as much for Dog as for himself was stilled only when Josh Mason, followed by a brood of boys as tall and rangy as himself, walked over. First he clapped Callum on the shoulder, then he knelt down and stroked Dog, talking all the while to Rory about how he'd never seen such a fine, brave animal, protecting its master like that.

Dog butted Mason with her head and he stroked her with renewed vigor, causing her tail to thump. Wee Dougal came running and jumped on her broad back. He was soon joined by Mason's youngest. The small boys and the huge dog rolled and wrestled, then Dog, with the two boys astride her, wove her way among the tables, panting.

Other small children began clamoring for such rides, ignoring their parents' reluctance. Callum soon found himself dragooned into the role of pony master. Dog bore all her riders, however much they wriggled or drummed their little heels against her sides, with forbearance.

Callum was amazed by Dog's sudden playfulness. He glanced over to where the man had fallen, prepared to be a sentinel in Dog's stead. He saw nothing but empty grass.

Chapter Six

The revelry continued late into the night. Major Nicholson's men brought out flambeaux to light the stubbled fields. Eli played his fiddle just as Rory had promised and, even if the airs he played were not the plaintive ones Callum knew, they made him think of home.

He remembered how his father used to play for him and his mother on quiet evenings. Whenever he played, he closed his eyes, his long, thin body swaying to the sweet music that poured from the fiddle. Callum's mother used to tease him, saying this was his true nature being revealed, the one usually kept hidden by the fusty black of his minister's garb and the rules and precepts of the kirk. She would sigh and reminisce about the young man she'd first met, the one who had wooed her with music and song. As her frailty had increased and the lines of worry had engraved themselves deeply on his face, the fiddle playing had become less frequent, until it stopped altogether. Callum wondered what had become of his father's fiddle.

No trace of it was found when Mrs. Lennie had helped him sort out his father's belongings when he had to leave the manse. Indeed, Callum could not recall his father playing it once since his mother's death.

Trude and Rory kept their children close by, and Callum was introduced to so many people that his head was filled fit to buzzing with all their names and the questions they asked him. Even if he had not been cast upon center stage by Dog and her antics, Callum knew he would have been the focus of everyone's attention, so hungry were people for news from what was, for many, the Old Country. Tonight, though, it was curiosity about Dog that flamed at least half the questions. After an initial reluctance to tell the strange way in which he had acquired her, Callum found himself acting it out with gusto. The story was greeted with oohs and ahs of wonder as well as much tutting at the behavior of Dog's former owner. In the telling, Callum even found himself showing people the carved box — although he never let anyone touch it, not even when they begged to do so.

The first time Callum started to tell his story, Rory whispered out of the corner of his mouth, "Leave out how much you paid for her. They'll think we're all touched if they but knew!"

Callum's audience was appreciative and he was amused, later on, to hear the tale being passed around by others. Dog was quickly assuming mythical proportions and magical powers. As one gossip told it, "Big the beast was, swelled to the size of a horse with eyes like saucers that spun round and round. Back in England, where I come from, we had a dog like that, s'posed to haunt the hedgerows round Aylsham way. Black Shuck was what that old mawther was called." She had nodded her head sagely. "If we have beasties like this in the Old Country, why mayn't there be ones here in this wild land?" When her audience nodded agreement, she had continued, casting a wary glance at Dog. "But this 'un is more gentle like. Look how she plays with the little boys and maids!"

Josh Mason's family stayed nearby, and Callum found himself thrown in the company of Amy, Mason's daughter. Callum was surprised to find that she was thirteen, two years younger than himself. She seemed older, and he gathered from her manner in dealing with her unruly brothers, and from snippets of conversation, that she ran the household. This was confirmed when she started talking about family. "Have you no other relatives at all, saving Big Rory?"

Unused to such directness, Callum stared into the darkness and mumbled, "My father's brothers are dead, long since. Their fishing boat went down with all hands. There's other half brothers and sisters on my mother's side, but my mother had cut herself off from them long before she died. They wanted nothing to do with the get of a

Protestant." Bitterness flooded Callum's mouth as though the words were something bad tasting and foul. His eyes felt hot and prickly and his hand sought the reassurance of Dog's solid presence as she lay beside him on the ground.

Pausing only to straighten out the crumpled limbs of her youngest brother, who lay sprawled across her lap asleep, Amy said, in a tone that shocked Callum with its matter-of-factness, "Has your ma been dead long then? Mine died birthing this one here, nigh on three years ago now."

"But who looks after you all?" Callum blurted out.

Amy laughed, so loudly that her small brother woke and began to grizzle. "Well, I do of course. Who else is there?" She positioned her brother so that his head nestled on her shoulder and gently rocked him until he quietened.

Callum pictured how hard his aunt worked looking after the seven of them and mentally counted the Masons. Amy had five brothers. "But you're just a girl!"

Amy's tone was amused. "I helped Ma since I could toddle behind her. I knew what had to be done and Pa sets the littler boys to help me when he has no need for them in the fields." With her free hand, she pushed wisps of brown hair behind her ears. When she spoke again, her voice was filled with excitement. "I love the harvest supper! It's a rare treat to hear music and meet people." She giggled and blushed. "This must seem dull though, to you, Callum, coming from halfway across the world, from a big city. Oh, the things you must have seen!" Amy sighed and her voice was wistful. "I've never been anywhere but Coote's Paradise. Pa and Ma came here soon after the Revolution. They'd been run off their farm in New York. Pa was away fighting, but Ma and the two big boys built us a home and a farm, 'something for him to come back to,' she said."

"We were the first family to settle here. It's only in the last ten years that others have come. Big Rory came but four years ago, and brought Trude and the children a year later." She smiled. "Oh, that did gladden Pa's heart! Rory and Caleb, my oldest brother of all, were of an age at the start of the war." Amy's smile faltered. "I never knew Caleb, though. He died then." She turned so she faced Callum, her large hazel eyes glowing, as her thoughts veered again to the present. "Why, we even have an inn and a mill now. Soon we'll be a proper town. Won't that be grand?"

The enormity of what Amy had just said struck Callum dumb. A kaleidoscope of images shifted in his head: the tall jumbled tenements of Edinburgh; the grand buildings of New Town; the tumbledown fishers' cottages; the dark, cramped bowels of the boat that brought him to the Canadas; the new, proud buildings of York; and everywhere people in all their differences, haggling in the market, working, sweating, vomiting and, above all else, talking, laboring to make something of their lives. He swallowed, struggling to find words that expressed how he felt about how fortunate he had been, how he could not imagine living a life so circumscribed as that which Amy accepted so readily. A ragged moan escaped from deep inside as Callum realized this was now his life, too, unless he had the courage to strike out on his own, isolated and friendless in a country that was not his own.

Looking directly at Callum, Dog whined, a thin, silvery sound that cut through the warm night air. The whine rose, gaining in volume until it was a full-throated howl.

"Whisht your noise!" Rory's voice was harsh as he came running from where he had been talking to Amy's father.

Dog fell silent immediately, but she remained staring at Callum, her eyes flashing green in the reflected torchlight.

"Callum, what are you thinking of, letting Dog make herself a spectacle again? Can ye not see that people are staring? Have we not already convinced everyone that we are fey?" Rory shook his head, then noticed how Callum trembled at his side. "Ach, laddie, what ails you?"

When Callum was unable to answer, unable to express how overwhelmed he felt, Rory gently steered him to where Josh Mason and Trude waited, sleeping children in their arms. As they walked,

Rory kept up a loud, one-sided conversation. "It's been a long and hard day's work for all, especially for those of us unused to such toil. I think it's time to set out for home. We all still have chores to do on the morrow. We've eaten and drunk well, danced and sung, for which I thank you," he said, with a nod of acknowledgment to Major Nicholson, who sat like a king on a chair his servants had positioned on a small rise. "Let's hope the weather holds for us and that our own harvests will be so bountiful!"

Although people still stared at Callum and Dog as they passed, most took Rory's words as the signal to start their own leaving, and Callum was able to lose himself in the hustle and bustle. Of Rory's brood, only Sandy was still awake, if only by willpower. As soon as he was safely in the bed of the wagon, his eyes closed.

As Callum waited for Dog to jump into the wagon, he felt a hand upon his arm. Amy Mason stood behind him, her small face troubled.

"If I gave offense, I'm sorry." She wryly smiled. "Ma always used to say I was a hasty speaker."

Callum forced himself to speak, surprised by how important it was to him that Amy not feel herself to be the cause of his distress. He was struck by the strange notion that, although their color was quite different, her eyes had the same gentleness as Dog's. "No, no ... the music ... it made me think of home."

"Callum!" Trude called from the seat of the wagon. "Let's be off."

Hastily jumping up, Callum found a space for himself between Dog and the backboard.

With a click of his tongue, Rory set the oxen in motion. As they passed him, Josh Mason turned from settling his smallest boy and shouted, "Think on, Rory, about my proposal, won't you?"

"Aye, I will," Rory replied and then concentrated on guiding the oxen through the knots of people.

"What proposal?" Trude sounded curious.

"Something and nothing. We'll talk of it later." Rory's tone brooked no argument, and Callum felt a pang of disappointment. He had liked Mason and would like to see more of him and his family.

Trude was staring at Callum and Dog. He dreaded the questions that he knew must be churning in her head, so he closed his eyes and feigned sleep.

Dog had fallen asleep almost instantly and now was beset by a dream. Callum felt her legs hit his as she made running motions, but he struggled to keep his eyes closed.

Trude's voice floated back. "There's something uncanny about that animal. People will be talking for months about her. If she was not so good with the children, I'd not be happy with her presence about the place. What say you, Rory?"

Rory grunted. "Aye. More and more I'm convinced she's not what she seems, but she is young

Callum's mainstay. I'll not take that from him. That boy's had too much taken from him already."

Callum felt peace flood through him and sleep claimed him.

> ➤ ➤ ➤

After the late night, Callum had hoped Rory would sleep in, but his hoarse whisper floated up to the sleeping loft the next morning, before the sun had risen. Even Sandy, who usually leaped eagerly from his bed, moved slowly, and Callum felt as if his limbs were made of lead as he dragged himself down the ladder to start the day. Only Dog had energy, frisking as if some huge burden had been lifted. Callum spoke sharply to her when she almost tripped him. She looked resentfully at him and whined, her head cocked to one side as if puzzled by his sour mood.

Rory was all business when the boys staggered outside to the barn. "We made good money yesterday. Now we have enough to buy another cow, but there'll be no point in having that if we don't have hay to feed her or wheat for ourselves. So we've got to get our own harvest in while the weather holds." He pointed at the heavy dew that coated everything. "Yon's a good sign that we'll have fine weather awhile yet. We need that for the hay to dry. I'll sharpen the sickles and my scythe, while you boys feed and water the animals. Be quick about it, we need an early start. As it is, we'll be working all day, and then we'll still have the wheat to do."

Even breakfast was rushed and as they ate, Rory was giving instructions, detailing who would do what. Only Sandy's protestations that he was man enough to cut roused Callum from his gloom. He didn't see why his cousin was so unhappy; bringing water to the field seemed far easier than cutting the hay. He remembered how tired and sweaty Rory, Josh Mason and he had been at the end of the day's cutting yesterday.

Callum's irritation increased once they got started. Rory insisted on showing him how to use a sickle again, despite his avowals that Mason had already shown him. Only a growl from Dog and a nudge from her nose made him focus on what Rory was saying.

"Watch out for tree stumps, Callum." Rory's voice sounded concerned. "We don't have the luxury of Major Nicholson, every field cleared and plowed. If ye hit one, the sickle could bounce back and catch you in the leg, and that's something no one wants to happen. I'll take the scythe — there's a knack to that. You should be safer with the sickle. If you do come to a stump or rock, cut round it carefully."

Callum was taking a few practice swings, already conscious of how much his back would ache at the end of a day stooping to use the small sickle, when an exclamation from Rory made him start, and he narrowly missed Dog. The sickle's blade passed inches from her head.

"Watch out for birds and animals. They hide in the roots and can give a man a nasty shock when they leap out."

Callum pulled a face, making sure that neither Dog nor Rory saw.

Callum had often heard Rory complain about the smallness of his fields but, to him now, they seemed endless. In order to ignore the ache that had already lodged in his back and shoulders, Callum recited poetry in his head. Everyone seemed to have their own way of dealing with the monotony of the work. Dog ranged ahead and alongside, always mindful of the sharp blades, and it became apparent that she was driving out any birds or animals that had not yet fled at their approach. Trude talked continually to Dougal and Alison, who trailed behind her, Alison carrying wee Jamie. Rory sang, his fine deep voice rising into the sunshine:

> I like to rise when the sun she rises,
> Early in the morning.
> I like to hear those small birds singing,
> Happily at the dawning.
> Oh, for the life of a country plowboy,
> Rambling through the new-mown hay!

The cheerful aptness of the words, which Rory repeated over and over, finally became too much for Callum, and he began to sing in competition, an old song his mother had loved dearly, one that she said their nurse had sung to her and Rory. As Callum's thin tenor, still occasionally cracking, sang of the great silkie of Sule Skerrie, Rory smiled, left off his own song and joined in. As their voices rang out, Callum felt a great surge of happiness, a sense of belonging that suddenly made his sickle seem like a feather in his hand. When the song ended, he laughed aloud and shouted to Rory, "Again, Uncle!"

"Aye, laddie." Rory's beard was almost split in two by the breadth of his smile as he sang the first verse — a smile that vanished abruptly when Dog bulleted out of the long grass, almost bowling Callum over. "Good God! What's the matter with the beast now?"

Dog planted herself in front of Callum, staring intently at him. She yipped, a stream of little barks as if she was encouraging him.

"What? What do you want?" Callum was puzzled.

Dog yipped again and when Callum still did not respond, she made a yodeling sound.

Rory's shock turned to amusement. He leaned on the handle of his scythe. "She's singing. I swear she's singing."

Trude, who had stopped work, too, shivered. "If that's what she's doing, she's too knowing by half. She fair makes my skin crawl."

Dog was still making the strange noise, still staring eagerly at Callum as if willing him to respond to her in some way.

Rory broke in when Dog paused. "I think she wants you to sing, Callum. Go on, sing the next verse."

Feeling more than a little foolish, Callum started on the second verse:

I am a man upon the land,
I am silkie on the sea,
And when I'm far and far frae land,
My hame it is in Sule Skerrie.

This was evidently what Dog wanted, for she barked, a joyous sound so loud that Trude clapped her hands to her ears. Then, frisking like a puppy, Dog gamboled around Callum while the others watched in stunned amazement.

Finally, when Dog subsided into a happy panting heap, Trude, looking from Callum to Rory, said, "I know that's one of your old Scots ballads, but what does it mean and why is the beast so taken with it?"

Rory was amused. "I can answer your first question, my dear. A silkie is a creature who is a seal, like any other, but far cleverer, because when it's on land, it sheds its skin and becomes a man. As to why yon strange beastie likes it so well, I ken not. What about you, Callum?"

Callum shook his head. He felt he should be able to make a connection but it eluded him.

"Ah well," Rory said, "with Dog, we have surprises each day, but time's a'wasting. Let's get back to work."

And that they did, working the whole day, until Callum was sure he would never be able to move his arms again. By evening both fields were cut and the hay had been spread to bake in the sun, which they prayed would continue to shine for several more days.

Throughout the day, Callum had been aware that his aunt and uncle had been deep in conversation whenever they thought themselves in no danger of being overheard. Twice, he had moved nearer in the hope of hearing whatever was causing such serious discussion, but on seeing him approach, they had either fallen silent or Rory had burst into song. Despite having failed to hear anything, Callum had the feeling their conversation concerned him. He had sensed his aunt staring at him in a way he could only describe as speculative. At first, he had fretted, fearing Trude's unease about Dog and her strange ways was growing and that she was trying to convince Rory to send her on her way. Then he recalled his uncle's words in the wagon, calling Dog Callum's "mainstay," and he knew Rory was not a man who spoke lightly. Callum even tried asking Sandy, as they bedded down the animals for the night, if he knew what was bothering his parents.

Sandy shrugged. "I'm not sure," he said, "but it *is* about you, that's for certain." A slow smile tweaked the corners of Sandy's mouth. "Mebbe," he said, drawing out his words with obvious pleasure, "they're going to hire you out for a servant. Mebbe Major Nicholson's boy needs his own manservant."

Callum paled at the thought of being bound in such a way, of working for that lout who had neither manners nor any interest in learning. He started to protest until he recognized the spark of mischief in Sandy's eyes.

"Ha, ha! You nearly believed me, didn't you?" Sandy was cock-a-hoop at having tricked Callum. "Dadda would never do anything like that, as well you should know by now. Whatever it is, Mammie was all for it, whilst Dadda wasn't sure. That's all I heard before they realized that I was listening, but they did say that they'd tell us all after supper."

To Callum, supper that night seemed to last forever, even though it was just a cold collation of sliced meat, bread and cheese, as Trude had been working in the fields all day. Although he was hungry, he found it hard to sit still, and his agitation transferred itself to Dog, who paced restlessly. Wee

Jamie was slow to settle and his crying kept Dougal awake, so it was late before the rest of the family settled around the fire. Unusually, for it was their custom to be abed when dark fell, Trude lit some precious candles and set them around the hearth.

Alison, already in her nightgown, clambered onto her father's knee and asked, "Are we to have stories tonight, Dadda?"

Rory patted her head, drawing her close to his chest. "Mebbe later, my flower, but first, your mother and I have something we want to discuss with your big cousin, Callum."

Callum's heart beat faster. He stroked Dog's fur and she leaned against him as he scanned Rory's face for some clue as to what it was that was being treated with such seriousness. It could be nothing too bad, he concluded, for he could see, in the dim light, the familiar wrinkles around Rory's eyes that came when he smiled.

Trying to sound calm, he said, "Oh, aye, and what might that be, Uncle?"

Trude and Rory looked at each other, as if deciding who should speak. Finally, Rory said, "Callum, would ye fancy being a schoolteacher?"

Callum felt as if someone had sucked all the air out of his body. He wanted so badly to speak, to say that this was one of his dreams, but nothing came out for some seconds, until he was eventually able to splutter, "But how? Where?"

Rory clapped his hands on his knees and laughed out loud at Callum's discomfiture. "Do I gather that you're not overfond of farm work then, young Callum, so pleased are you to be offered alternative employment?"

"Yes. No. I don't mean to sound ungrateful." Callum struggled to say the right thing.

Rory leaned over and gave him a gentle cuff around the head. "It's all right, laddie, we know the work has been hard and foreign to you, but you've done your best. A man can't ask for more than that." He smiled over Alison's head at Trude. "It's Josh Mason's idea. He's been after me for a while to teach the bairns." He turned his grin on Callum. "You heard him yourself yesterday. The man's got a bee in his bonnet about it, but I havnae the time. Well, he wondered if you would do it."

His thoughts whirling, Callum prayed that there were practical solutions that he had not been able to work out. "Where would I have the time, Uncle? Would the children come here?"

Trude spoke for the first time. "It would be in town, Callum. Only during the winter months, mind, for we could do with your help in the planting season and through the summer till harvest. Eli has said that you can use his back room at the inn. The children would come in as long as the weather holds."

Rory broke in then. "Those of us who have

books will lend them, and you'll get paid as well. Not in money, I'm afraid, but in whatever people can spare. I won't lie to you, Callum — what you would earn would help us out, too. The farm is still new, and I've not yet cleared and worked the acreage that others have."

Rory's words washed over Callum. A schoolmaster, a dream that he thought was lost to him forever! He realized Rory was staring at him anxiously. "I'm sorry, Uncle," he said. "I didnae catch what you said."

"Well, Callum, what's your answer to be?"

Laughter surged inside Callum like bubbles in water.

Both Trude and Rory looked at him in amazement. Alison started to giggle, too, and it wasn't long before Sandy joined in, so infectious was Callum's happiness.

"Nephew, I'm assuming that this means you will take it on?" Rory tried to sound stern, but with Alison squirming on his lap, he was fighting down a chuckle.

"Oh, aye, Uncle, that it does."

Chapter Seven

Elation carried Callum through the rest of the hay harvest, even though the work was tedious and muscle straining. The hot weather, with which they were blessed, left him perpetually drenched in sweat. With the prospect of returning to his beloved books, of sharing them with others, of even being paid to do so, but most of all of not having to labor on the farm, Callum felt a happiness he had not known since before he made the long trip from Scotland. His good temper and high spirits made many of the chores seem to fly by; and he, Rory and Sandy worked well alongside one another. They often sang, taking pleasure in teaching Sandy the Gaelic songs and laments they both loved so well. Although nothing was ever said, Rory and Callum chose never to sing of the great silkie again.

In contrast to Callum's newfound peace, Dog seemed unsettled and fretful. More and more often, when Callum was busy, it became obvious that something else claimed her attention.

Even Sandy noticed, and he couldn't resist teasing Callum. "Looks like you've lost your nursemaid, Callum." When Callum had looked puzzled, Sandy continued, "She hovered over you making sure you got things right. Why, Dadda said that had she but hands instead of paws, he would have had one of the best workers in the whole of Upper Canada! Mebbe she thinks you know what you're doing now. Me, though," and here Sandy giggled, "I still think you're a gowk!"

Dog did leave Callum to his own devices more. He felt a small puff of pride that he was no longer "a whey-faced city boy who didn't know one end of a cow from the other." He started to watch Dog and soon began to detect a pattern to her behavior. Most of the time she stared into the far distance, her eyes scanning the horizon as if she was searching for something or someone. Previously, she had remained as close by Callum's side as was practical, but now she ranged restlessly, sometimes until she was but a black dot on the horizon.

The first time this happened, Callum panicked. Dropping his rake and running carelessly through the lines of dried hay he had been piling for collection, he yelled, "Dog! Dog! Get back here!" When she paid no heed, remaining on the far side of the cabin where the woods were not yet cleared, Callum pelted to her side, arriving with dry mouth and heaving chest. He felt inside his shirt for the wooden box.

Before he could speak, Dog turned to him, whimpered and looked back into the darkness between the trees.

Callum peered into the blackness but saw nothing. "What is it, girl? What do you see? Or want to see?"

Dog whimpered again and slowly plodded back to where Callum had been working. Her head hung and her thick plume of a tail drooped so low that it brushed the ground. She threw herself down, her head on her paws, muzzle turned toward the woods.

Dog's wanderings became commonplace, and once Callum realized that all he had to do to ensure her return was to touch the wooden box, he no longer felt the stomach-churning fear that he would lose her. He noticed she was drawn to the line where cultivated land met forest or water. So, in his precious moments of free time, Callum made sure to walk in the woods so Dog could roam where she obviously yearned to be. Sometimes Sandy accompanied them, and for this Callum was grateful — the darkness of the forest still made him uneasy. His rational mind could not banish the fey creatures that populated the woods and waters according to his mother's stories. Trude's stories — of her life near Albany and how her family believed in the little creatures who lived in the surrounding woods and who delighted in tricking travelers — confirmed that such things could occur in the Americas, too. Indeed, the wildness of the landscape and the lack of people made it all the more likely to Callum.

After such rambles, Dog seemed calmer. The only times she frolicked or seemed happy were when she rough-and-tumbled with the little children, especially Jamie, who by the end of the summer was taking his first tottering steps on legs that looked too fat and bowed to hold him.

Jamie adored Dog, and she allowed him liberties that would have drawn a warning growl had anyone else made so free with her person. He climbed all over her, pulled her tail and ears when he was not crooning baby babble into them. Sometimes, he rode her like a pony, and other times, he used her as a pillow, falling asleep with his face pressed into her side as his parents worked in the fields. Callum felt a pang of jealousy on such occasions.

After the hay had been dried and stored in the barn, Rory drove them all to bring the wheat in safely. Callum did not mind the harvesting itself, but the threshing and winnowing of the grain, which raised great clouds of dust and chaff in the closed quarters of the barn, seemed to drag on forever. He reminded himself again and again that soon he would be free of all this, working in a clean room, teaching students eager to learn. This, however, did little to lessen the way the chaff stuck to his sweaty skin and found its way into his eyes, causing them to itch unmercifully. It was then he wished for a brownie to help them. He closed his eyes, imagining coming down in the morning to find all the chores done by the little familiar spirit of the Highland, who required nothing more than a bowl of cream for his labors.

One day, Callum and Sandy were working by themselves. Rory had gone to visit Josh Mason, and Callum was feeling particularly out of sorts because Rory had refused his request to go to Mason's, too.

"Och, Callum," Rory had said, his eyes kind as he looked at his nephew. "I'd sorely love the company, for it's a tedious ride, but if I take you, then Sandy would want to come, and then Alison." A gesture with one hand indicated that, before he knew it, he'd have the whole family packed in the wagon. "We'd lose a day's work, and we cannae afford that, not with our winter preparations to make." Seeing Callum's obvious disappointment, Rory joked, "Now is it the novelty of a trip, or is there some deeper reason for your eagerness, young Callum? Would it have anything to do with a certain young lady with whom you spent so much time at the harvest supper?"

Callum started to protest, but was stunned to find himself blushing. He had not realized it, but he would dearly love to see Amy Mason again. He liked the way in which she said what she thought, the way she had been so concerned about his feelings.

"Callum's sweet on Amy! Callum's sweet on Amy!" Sandy chanted, capering in an annoying way. The chant was soon picked up by Alison, and Callum had to fight to control his temper, although he knew they meant no real harm.

"Now see what you've started," Trude scolded. "Be off with you, Rory MacBean, while I calm these hooligans down." Laying a hand on Callum's arm, she said, "Take no notice, Callum. There's nothing wrong with liking someone, and Amy Mason is one of the sweetest girls I've known, and," she added, "one of the most uncomplaining and hardworking."

"Uncomplaining" and "hardworking," those words rang in Callum's head for the rest of the day. Hardworking he had certainly become, but uncomplaining? Callum winced. Although he rarely voiced any complaint, complaints were never far from his thoughts. He resolved to try to be more positive in his outlook, especially since he would soon be free of the chores that he found so draining.

Such resolve, however, did not prevent him from reacting excitedly to Rory's return late in the afternoon. As soon as he heard the creak of the oxen's harness outside the barn, Callum dropped his end of the winnowing tray, heedless of Sandy's cry of outrage and pain as it landed on his feet, and ran outside to greet his uncle. He fussed around the oxen, unbuckling their harness and wishing that Trude would cease questioning Rory about whom he had seen on the way so that he could ask whether anything had been said about when the school would start. Finally, he got his chance.

"Uncle, was Mr. Mason pleased that you've agreed to my teaching?" Callum was proud that he used such subtlety, although his tongue burned to ask when he might start.

Rory led the oxen toward the water trough, taking care to give Dog, who had followed Callum out from the barn, a wide berth. The oxen no longer balked at the sight of her, but they were still uneasy if she was too close. "Aye, that he was, Callum. He's spoken to most of the other families and nearly all of them are agreeable and will be sending their bairns of an age to learn." Rory smiled to see how happiness glowed from Callum's face. He added, "I know it's what you long for, laddie, but it might not be all that you dream of. Some of those who'll be there are the same age as yourself. Van Every's boy is older. They might not take kindly to being taught by one such as yourself, however clever." When he saw no change in Callum's expression, Rory continued, his voice slow and deliberate as if to pound his point home. "They are wild ruffians, some of them, used to being their own masters. It's no going to be easy."

Still beaming, Callum said, "Och, I'll manage, Uncle, dinna fret." He could contain himself no longer. "When will I start?"

Shaking his head, but seeing no point in more warnings, Rory led the oxen back to the barn now that their thirst had been slaked. Over his shoulder, he said, "We thought the end of October. I'll need your help with clearing brush till then, getting in a good supply of firewood. Mebbe we'll even slaughter and dress the pigs before you go. Your pupils will be busy till then, too."

Callum heard nothing after "the end of October." Somehow, he had thought that once the wheat was safely stored or taken to the mill, all work was done and Rory would manage on his own, as he had always done. Callum had expected to leave in days, and here it was only the beginning of September. He had eight long weeks before he would be free.

Sensing his distress, Dog nuzzled Callum's hand, her tongue rough and warm.

Angrily, Callum pulled away. He ran back into the barn, grabbing hold of the winnowing tray, yelling at Sandy to get back to work. Tears made a very good defense against chaff in the eyes.

That evening at supper, Rory was in fine form, recounting his day's adventures at the Mason farm. He laughed as he told Trude and the children how Josh, while they had worked together constructing a new byre, had spent most of the day extolling the virtues of buying sheep rather than the extra cow that Rory had in mind.

Trude smiled. "Well, Rory, our own wool would be nice, instead of having to trade with the Widow Dagget for it. I swear she drives her flock through the biggest mud puddles she can find before she shears them. I always spend twice as long washing her fleeces as I did back in Albany. I sometimes think that there is more grit and mud than actual wool!"

Callum glowered as he listened to the good-natured banter that swirled around him. Even Dog's affectionate presence did not lighten his mood as resentment built inside him. A small, nagging voice that would not be stilled muttered inside his head: *If it wasn't for me and my labor, they'd not even be thinking of new livestock.* Sour thoughts like these plagued him all evening, and he was glad when it was time for bed, even though he remained awake.

Lying in the dark of the loft, listening to Sandy's easy breathing and Dog's occasional whimpers, Callum came up with a plan that he hoped might hasten his departure for town.

The next morning dawned fair, although there was a definite crispness to the air. Callum was grateful for the warmth of Dr. Lennie's old coat, which he had not worn since his arrival in Coote's

Paradise. Rory announced they would start clearing more land, stockpiling firewood for the long winter, when they might not venture out of the cabin if the snow was deep. Callum smiled, thinking of his plan, although Rory took it to mean that he looked forward to the day's work, chiding Sandy for not showing similar enthusiasm.

Sandy protested, "Och, Dadda, it's all right for Callum. He gets to do interesting stuff. I'll bet he'll even get to use the ax." The reverence in Sandy's voice made Callum smile even more, and he couldn't resist teasing his cousin by miming using an ax. Sandy continued his complaint. "All I ever get to do is to gather up the branches and the brush. You don't even let me use the wee hatchet." He stood there, his hands on hips, a scowl twisting his features, appearing so comical that both Rory and Callum laughed.

"Ah, Sandy, don't be in such a hurry to grow up." Rory's voice was gentle. "You'll have time enough for all the hard labor, isn't that right, Callum?"

Callum's laughter stopped instantly and his face became set and sullen. "Aye," was all he said, although all his thoughts centered on how little hard labor he would have to do, if things worked out as he hoped.

"Come here, Sandy." Rory ruffled his son's hair. "Felling trees is not an easy task. It takes practice and strength. I'll be teaching Callum today. Your turn will come in time. And as for using the ax, well, you know how I feel about that ax! It was given to your dadda by the Crown when we first settled here, along with my saw." Rory's smile became rueful and he shook his head. "Who'd have thought that I'd treasure something given to me by the damn English? But it's precious because it marks me as a man who owns his own land — something I thought would never come about."

Shouldering the ax and handing Callum the whipsaw, Rory moved off, indicating that all discussion was over. The two boys and Dog trailed after him to the edge of the forest, where Rory examined the trees, finally settling upon a tall maple. He set Sandy and Callum to clearing the brush from around its base. Spitting upon his hands, he gripped the ax firmly, swinging it with all his might against the trunk. The ax bit into the trunk with a solid *ker-chunk*. He continued to swing the ax rhythmically, all the while instructing Callum on the finer points of felling a tree: the necessity of maintaining a firm grip on the handle at all times, how the injury any settler dreaded was a gash from an ax, how to ensure the tree fell in the direction that did the least damage.

Callum fizzed and fumed with impatience, barely listening to Rory's words. Even handling the ax seemed preferable to the little boy make-work that Rory had set him, although what he really longed to do was to sit in front of the fire with a book. Rory had returned yesterday with a copy of Mr. Wordsworth's *Lyrical Ballads* that Eli at the inn had lent him when he stopped for ale, and Callum was itching to read it.

After what seemed like an age, Rory handed Callum the ax and pointed to where he was to chop. Callum hefted the ax, surprised at how heavy it was. He brought it up behind his shoulders and prepared to swing it. The speed of the ax's downward momentum took him by surprise. To his horror, he felt the smooth handle slide from his grip. Callum grunted as he struggled to hold on, unaware that Sandy had moved behind him, slightly to one side, the better to see how Callum fared.

As if it was greased with butter, the ax handle slithered from Callum's grasp. The ax hit the tree trunk, bounced off and flew backward straight at Sandy. Callum's anguished cry was echoed by a great roar that ripped from the very depths of Rory's chest.

A black blur launched itself from the ground and Dog's two front paws thudded into Sandy's chest, knocking him backward as the ax passed through the space where he had stood. He lay winded on the ground, Dog lying protectively on top, the ax embedded in the rich loam a short distance away.

Callum lurched toward his cousin and Dog, sinking to his knees at their side. Great gulping sobs racked him as he reached out a tentative hand, which was brushed aside by Rory, who roughly hoisted Dog back on her paws.

Rory's ruddy complexion had drained of color. Gently lifting Sandy, Rory held him close to his chest, cradling his head and rocking him as he did wee Jamie, his lips moving, although Callum could not make out what it was he muttered. Only when Sandy began to cough and struggle did Rory loosen his grip, holding him at arm's length as if to confirm what his eyes could see — Sandy was shocked but unhurt.

Callum remained kneeling, an arm gratefully draped around Dog's broad shoulders. "Uncle," he stuttered, his voice sounding raw in his ears. "I didnae ... I didnae ken Sandy was there ..."

Rory's face was now a deep, brick red. A vein in his neck pulsed, standing out like a snake amongst the tendons. "You bluidy young fool!" he bellowed at Callum. "You almost killed Sandy! I told you to keep a firm grip, did I not?" Rory spat the words out. "Did you listen? No. You were too busy lollygagging, lost in your own selfish thoughts."

Callum flinched at Rory's words. A deep overpowering shame welled up inside him. In his mind's eye, he saw what might have been: Sandy's blond hair matted with blood, his body lying limp in the brush. Tears started to his eyes again, and he felt snot run from his nose. Words lodged in his throat like lumps of gristle between sobs. "Uncle, I'm so sorry. I never meant ... I'd not hurt Sandy for the world."

Rory rocked back on his heels, seeming to sink in on himself. He did not look at Callum when he spoke again, his voice quieter. One hand absently stroked Sandy's hair. "I know that, laddie, but —" Rory pounded the ground with his free hand. "Och, I cannae think. All I see is that bluidy ax flying through the air and Sandy. If it hadnae been for Dog ..." He paused, took a deep breath. "Just go."

Callum's sobs stopped. He looked at Rory, uncertain of his meaning.

"Go, I said!" Rory bellowed so loudly that Sandy set up a thin wail. "Just stay out of my sight for the rest of the day."

Callum was so shocked he did not move. Dog grabbed his sleeve in her teeth and pulled. He staggered to his feet, pulling free from her grip. He started to speak, but then thought better of it. Dog had already set off into the woods and Callum ran after her, as fast as he could.

Ignoring the branches and undergrowth that tugged and tore at him, Callum ran and ran. At first, his feet echoed the pounding of his heart, but gradually he found comfort in the monotony of placing one foot in front of the other, the solid rhythmic thunks keeping the images of Rory and Sandy from filling his head.

Callum was only vaguely aware that Dog paced him, slowing her powerful lope so that she remained at his side. For a brief stretch, the running took on an ease that surprised him: his breath came easily, filling his lungs with coolness; his limbs flowed with power; and he felt that he could run until he reached the very ocean. But his legs became heavy, his chest filled with molten lead, and the earth suddenly tilted and came rushing toward Callum who welcomed its dark, damp embrace.

How long he lay there, Callum never knew. Once his breath came back, he cried — a silent wash of tears. Then he lost himself in darkness, never sure whether it was sleep or something else. When he came to, Dog was standing over him, straddling his body with her own, her muzzle a hairsbreadth from his face. Her breath was warm on Callum's face, her brown eyes glowing as she stared at him.

With exaggerated care, Dog stepped clear of him and sat by his side, her head cocked as if waiting for an answer.

Callum sat and drew his knees up, clasping his arms around them and resting his forehead on them to avoid Dog's fierce gaze. "No!" he finally burst out, and he raised his head to meet Dog's stare. "I swear it wasnae deliberate."

Dog whined, shifting uneasily.

"I dinna know how it's possible, but I know you know my thoughts." Callum took Dog's muzzle in his hands. His voice was low. "Och, I know I planned to be clumsy, to do my work in such a slipshod way that Uncle would be glad to see the back of me and send me off to town all the sooner, but I would never do ... something like that. I'd never hurt anyone." Callum tightened his grip, forcing Dog to look into his eyes. "You must believe me, Dog."

Finally, Dog wrested her muzzle free. Callum flinched slightly but did not move back as she licked his cheek.

Straightening up, Callum looked around him. He and Dog were in a small clearing. To one side, in the underbrush, there was the sign of his hurried entry in some broken branches and trampled ferns, but there were no other tracks or paths. Glimmers of sunlight rippled through the canopy of leaves. Callum stared upward.

"By the looks of that sun, we're not far off noon, Dog," Callum said. "We can't go back, not yet." His voice quavered and he fought against a sob. "I dread that. They'll all hate me, I know they will."

Dog butted Callum's leg with her head, but he took no notice.

"What'll Aunt Trude say when Uncle and Sandy tell her what I did? Perhaps they'll say I'm not fit to have the care of bairns if I almost kill my own cousin through carelessness!" With the heels of his hands, he ground the tears from his eyes. "Mebbe it's better if I never go back. If I die out here in the woods, eaten by wild animals, then they'll all be sorry!"

A crashing in the undergrowth on the other side of the clearing brought both Callum and Dog to their feet. With his last foolish words echoing in his head, Callum felt a wave of fear sweep over him. He reached down for Dog, only to find that she had moved toward the noise. Pictures of bears, fangs bared, claws poised to rend his flesh, threatened to overwhelm Callum, and he fought to retain control of his bladder, which suddenly seemed full to bursting. The noise was louder now and Callum knew that whatever was making it was no small animal.

Yet Dog's whole manner was calm and friendly. The hair on the back of her neck lay in its usual thick curls. Her tail was wagging. She suddenly let loose a volley of high-pitched, excited yips that jolted Callum from his fear.

Just as Callum moved toward her, a figure became visible at the edge of the clearing. It must be Rory — no one else was that tall. When the man stepped into the light, Callum's joy turned to apprehension, and for one terrible moment, all he saw were rows of tattooed dots writhing on sharp cheekbones. But this man could not be Dog's former owner, for all that he resembled him. This man had white, not black, hair.

Dog was frolicking around the stranger, dancing in circles, her tail wagging ever more furiously as she twisted and turned in an attempt to get as close as she could to him and lick his hands.

He knelt down and stroked her shoulders and flanks, talking softly in a language Callum did not understand. One word was repeated many times, "Airah," and every time the man said it, Dog barked.

Dog's reaction stilled Callum's fear, and he observed the stranger more closely. Now he saw that, although this man was tall, he was not as tall as Rory — only shadows and wishes had made him seem so. The white hair, cut in a crest that rose proudly from his head and flowed down his shoulders, was not the only sign of age. The man's skin was heavily weathered; the tattoos that had so scared Callum were almost lost in wrinkles. He was clothed in a way Callum had never seen: trews and shirt made out of some kind of soft animal skin and decorated with purple and white beading. Around his neck hung a carving, the flat shape of a dog — its head thrown back as it howled. The man appeared strong and hearty but it was a wiry strength that lacked Rory's bulk. He seemed to sense Callum's stare, for he tore his attention away from Dog, looked up and smiled at him.

"She's beautiful, your dog. Might I ask where you came by her?" The voice was gentle, accented in a way Callum found strange but pleasant.

Callum's first instinct was to turn and run, but instead he found himself smiling back and answering the man's question, recounting his acquisition of Dog with as much gusto and detail as he had at Major Nicholson's party.

Throughout Callum's story, the man nodded knowingly. His hands never left off stroking Dog's fur. When Callum finally fell silent, the man looked appraisingly at him. "You are hungry?" he asked. He didn't wait for an answer. "All boys your age are hungry," he stated, "just like all bears love berries." He reached to a skin pouch that hung behind his back. "Would you like to share my food while we talk more of this dog of yours?" The stranger sat down and pulled out some packages wrapped in corn husks, which he placed carefully on the ground in front of him.

Dog lay down at his side and Callum suddenly felt awkward standing, so he sank down, too, but at a certain distance because he still felt uneasy.

Inside the corn husks were strips of dried meat, some cold cornmeal studded with blueberries and even smoked fish. The stranger started off the meal by handing Dog some meat, which she took delicately from his fingers.

At first, Callum waited to be offered food, but his hunger surprised him and soon he was helping himself and eating heartily, encouraged by the stranger, whose pouch seemed bottomless — as soon as one portion was consumed another appeared.

When finally Callum was full, the man pulled out a waterskin. As Callum drank, the stranger started to talk again. "She is a good animal, this dog of yours?"

Puzzled by the way in which the question was phrased, Callum took his time in answering. "Aye, she's been a help around the farm" was his guarded reply.

"Tsk," the man sounded impatient, "all dogs, if they are trained properly, are helpful, but your dog is something more, no?"

Dog lifted her head at this and then laid it upon the man's knee, looking up into his face. A small sigh escaped from her.

Callum nodded and, almost against his will, told the man about the strangeness that was Dog: how she knew what he was thinking, sometimes before even he himself did; how she seemed to understand every word that was said; how the other farm animals were made uneasy by her. Last of all, with tears in his eyes, he told of how brave Dog was and how she had saved his cousin Sandy from Callum's foolishness and carelessness.

The man's face had remained impassive until the very end, and then he smiled, a smile that, although broad, seemed tinged with sadness. "She is brave, your dog, yes." When he spoke again, his eyes were fierce, and Callum squirmed when pinned by their gaze. "If you were ever asked to sell her, what would you say?"

"I have been already." Callum stopped, not wanting to describe the encounter with Dog's former owner. He felt himself turn red, as if the man knew he was holding something back. "But I refused. I'd never sell Dog!"

"Why are you so certain in your reply? If she is as special as you say she is, many a man would pay good money for such an animal."

Callum felt a twinge of irritation. Then he realized that Dog, too, was staring at him. He resolved to say no more, but the words were ripped from him. "She is my friend. My first friend. She has helped me make sense of this strange land." Callum turned his head away, shaken.

The old man was still and it was some time before he spoke. When he did, his voice was so low that Callum had to strain to make out the words, "Friendship is very powerful, but friendship can sometimes require sacrifice."

The old man gathered up the empty corn husks and packed them in his pouch. He placed both arms around Dog's neck and rested his forehead on hers, looking deep into her eyes. When the man finally broke the embrace and stood up, Callum was surprised to see that his eyes were wet and shiny.

In an effort to cover his embarrassment, Callum said, "But, sir, we've only spoken of me, my troubles and Dog. What of you? Do you live here, or are you passing through?" Callum was surprised at himself — he did not want the man to leave. "If the latter is the case, perhaps you would like to stay at my uncle's cabin this night?" Callum reddened, thinking that perhaps he had no right to make such an offer, but then he smiled. Whatever his anger at Callum, Rory was a gentleman who would not turn away anyone in need of shelter.

The old man shook his head, his crest of white hair rippling.

"You are a kind boy, if a troubled one. I would like to stay, but I have far to go." Reaching down to stroke Dog, the man continued, his voice wistful. "I am looking for my granddaughter."

"Does she live near here?" Callum was eager to help. "If she does, my uncle would be sure to know her, sir."

Sighing, the old man shook his head again. "She is lost and has been for many years."

The stranger's voice was so sad and resigned that Callum felt hollow inside. "If I meet a lost girl, sir, I'll tell her I've met you, that you're searching for her," Callum said, although he realized even as he spoke how empty and foolish his words were.

"She knows, boy. She knows." And the man drifted off into the trees.

Callum suddenly felt the urge to hold Dog. He placed his arms around her neck just as the old man had, but she was stiff and unyielding. He stood up and said, "Well, if that's how you feel, let's be finding our way out of this place."

Callum had taken but one step when a huge crashing came from the trees. Rory, with Sandy at his heels, came running into the clearing.

"Callum, Callum, we've found you!" Sandy yelled. "We've been looking all afternoon. Dadda's been so worried!"

A stew of emotions whirled inside Callum. Unwilling to lose control of them, he picked the obvious, the mundane. "But it's only just past lunchtime."

"You gowk, look at the light," Sandy said. And when Callum followed his pointing finger, he saw that the sky was the flaming orange of sunset.

"But," he said, "the man. Did you not see an old man? He went the way you came, and ..." Callum got no farther for Rory enveloped him in a crushing hug, into which he surrendered, savoring the warmth of his uncle's body, puzzled by why Rory was shaking.

When Rory finally released him, Callum repeated his question, a feeling he couldn't describe filling him.

Rory's voice was hoarse, as if he'd been shouting long and hard. "We saw no man, did we, Sandy? Just some kind of dog, a great old thing, brindled with age. I feared that you had encountered it and come to some harm."

Callum shivered.

"What ails you, Callum? What man?"

A bewilderment more intense than Callum had ever felt overcame him. There was a mystery here, one to which he had all the pieces, but whose pattern was teasingly unclear. He did not know what to say to Rory.

Dog began to prance, twirling round and round, until all who watched her felt dizzy. Then she howled.

Chapter Eight

As they walked through the darkening woods, Rory kept one arm around Callum's shoulders, whilst holding on to Sandy's hand with the other.

Callum was grateful. To his eyes, the trees looked twisted and malignant, seeming to close in on the three walkers. He was also grateful that his uncle had come to find him, that someone cared so much for him, after being on his own or in the care of strangers.

Sandy's natural exuberance was back as he recounted their search for Callum and Dog. It did much to banish the images of his limp form, brained by the ax, with which Callum had so tormented himself.

Rory talked of his fears: first, of what almost happened to Sandy; then, that his temper had driven Callum away and that he would be lost in the woods. "Ach, I blame myself, Callum," he said. "I was wrong to expect you to handle an ax like a man. You've been such a help of late that, mebbe, I expect too much."

Callum felt a pang of guilt at Rory's words. "No, Uncle," he protested, "I wasnae listening like I should." He paused, unsure of how to continue. "It's just that I get to thinking about being a schoolmaster, and I want it so badly that it all but fills my head and I get impatient, and ..."

"Aye, I know, laddie." Rory's voice was gentle and Callum had to strain to hear his next words. "When I was your age, I had dreams, too. To see the world, to be a fine chevalier. I saw myself in Paris or Rome, but the only way for me to leave the Highlands was to go with my uncle to America." A wistful note crept into Rory's voice. "If it hadnae been for the war, who knows?" When he spoke again, his booming tones echoed through the woods. "But if things had turned out differently, I wouldnae have my Trude or you bairns, would I now? We must all make the best of what we have, is that not right, boys?"

Touched by Rory's words, Callum felt the need to let Rory know this. "I swear that I'll work hard, Uncle, till it's time for me to go. I'll not daydream again, I promise."

"Aye, well I cannae ask for more than that, but don't promise the impossible, Callum. Everyone must have dreams. We just have to make time and care for the real world, too." Rory quickened his pace. "Let's get back and see what your aunt has for us. I hope it's some of her famous venison stew."

In the days that followed, as much as he was able, Callum was true to his word. He did work hard, listening attentively to Rory's instructions. Callum learned how to handle the ax competently if not skillfully, so that they cleared more land. He learned to handle Rory's musket when they went hunting, although the sight of a deer felled by a shot made him sick to his stomach — lithe grace reduced to mangled flesh and shattered bone.

Rory was right. Callum could not, however hard he tried, banish his daydreams. Physical work occupied Callum's body, but it gave his mind time to drift, and that it did. Often, when working alone, he imagined the bowed heads of industrious students as they produced page after page of fine script. He saw himself wallowing in the books lent to the school. From there it was but a small step to writing one himself — an account of his travails in Upper Canada, which would bring him both fame and fortune. He saw himself feted, first in York and then in London itself, where he would be invited to the finest salons and would astound everyone he met with his erudition and refinement. Many a time, Dog had to nudge him, and Callum would be surprised to find himself stiff from standing too long in one position, ignoring his chores.

With the date for his departure drawing ever closer, Callum became more distracted. Rory and

Callum had taken the oxen and cart out to the road. Sandy, despite his protests, had been left to help his mother. The day before had seen the end of the pigs, which had been fattened all summer long, and Callum was glad to leave the area around the cabin, which, to his nose, still reeked of blood. The squeals of the pigs had ripped through Callum, and he was glad that Rory did not expect him to help with the actual killing. It was all he could do to hold back vomit when he helped Rory manhandle their heavy carcasses as he butchered them. So it was with a great lightness of spirit that Callum greeted Rory's announcement that the two of them would spend some time cutting back the brush that grew along their frontage of the road to town and bring back the firewood.

There had been a heavy storm two days earlier, and when Callum and Rory reached the road, they saw what devastation had been done. A maple tree, a few leaves still clinging to its branches, had taken a direct hit from lightning, almost splitting its trunk in two. One half listed dangerously across the road.

"It'll have to come down, laddie," Rory said. "I thought we'd but spend the morning here, but it looks like we'll be here all day. Run to the cabin to tell your aunt and bring some food and water back with you." Rory lifted his ax out of the wagon. "I'll have it down by the time you return and you can help me saw it into logs."

With Dog loping at his heels, Callum set off at a run, relishing the freedom he had so unexpectedly been handed. It seemed to him but minutes before he was in the clearing where the cabin stood. There was no sign of anyone, and he hallooed until Sandy's head popped around the cabin's door.

"Has Dadda sent you to fetch me, 'cos he needs me after all?" Checking that his mother was not behind him, Sandy pulled a face and spat on the ground, glorying in the resounding splat. "She's got me chopping meat to make sausages. No matter how hard I try, the meat's never fine enough to suit her. I'll be glad to get away!"

Callum shook his head. "I'm afraid not, Sandy. You're stuck with the sausages." He added, "Just think how good they will taste," but Sandy stuck out his tongue and disappeared into the cabin.

Callum and Dog followed him in, to be confronted with a bustle of activity. Trude was cleaning the pigs' intestines for sausage skins. Sandy was chopping meat in a manner that made his annoyance very clear, while Alison chopped herbs. Even Dougal was busy, amusing Jamie by rolling a ball to and fro to him, so that he chortled and gurgled every time he managed to capture it between his clumsy baby hands. Callum explained as quickly as he could why he had returned and what Rory wanted.

Trude's face was flushed and she pushed strands of hair away from her face with the back of her hand. "There's a fresh loaf by the hearth, Callum. Take that and some cheese." She smiled. "Tell Rory it'll be sausage and onions tonight — it's his favorite."

Callum quickly did as he was told and took down a waterskin hanging by the door. "I'll not take water from the pail, Aunt," he said. "That way, you won't have to fetch more. It'll not take me but a minute to run down to the creek."

"Ah, you're a thoughtful boy, Callum," Trude said.

Callum felt a tiny twinge of guilt, for it had crossed his mind to take his ease for a few minutes in his favorite spot, reassuring himself that, before his arrival, Rory would have managed tree chopping and brush clearing by himself.

Although the day was cold, the sun shone and Callum found the creek a pleasant place, even without its canopy of leaves. The water sparkled as it ran over the stones, and Callum sat with his back against a tree trunk, idly skimming stones on the creek's surface. He only wished he had had the foresight to sneak a book into his coat pocket. As it was, he would have to make do with sinking into happy thoughts of life as a schoolmaster.

A thin, keening whine from Dog jolted Callum from his reverie. She was standing motionless, her fur bristling.

"What is it, Dog?" Callum was puzzled, but not alarmed, by her behavior. He had grown used to what Trude called Dog's "whims and fancies."

Dog turned troubled eyes toward him. Then she barked once, a deep bark that shook her whole frame. Leaving Callum staring stupidly, she headed through the trees in a direction that would not take her back to the cabin.

Throwing up his hands in exasperation, Callum took a last wistful glance at the peaceful waters of the creek, then set off after Dog. She was too far ahead to see, but he could hear her crashing sturdily through the brush, and her path was marked by flattened ferns and even broken branches, so swift and urgent was her run. At first, Callum jogged along, but when the sounds of her passage became faint, he ran in earnest, calling out her name between panting breaths.

When he saw the trees thinning out, Callum realized that Dog had led him to the road. He burst through the trees, quite prepared to berate her for her eagerness to return to work, but no words came when his eyes finally made sense of the scene before him.

At one side of the road, the oxen stamped their feet uneasily. One was lowing, a monotonous sound that drilled into Callum's brain. Only half of the lightning-blasted tree remained standing. Rory, his face white with pain, lay with his leg pinned under the other half.

"Callum, laddie, thank God you've come." Rory's voice was strained and he pushed himself up with his arms so that he was half sitting up. The movement caused a grimace of agony to twist his face and Callum rushed to his side.

"What happened, Uncle, why'd ye no wait for me?" Callum felt a surge of guilt rise as he thought of how slowly he had set about the task he had been given.

"Ach, it's such a bonny day that I knew you'd stop to savor it." Rory smiled at Callum, who struggled to meet his level gaze. "And I thought that if I but pulled on this old trunk, I'd bring it down in no time." Rory closed his eyes and leaned back. When he spoke again, his voice was rueful. "I didn't take into account the wet leaves, and I lost my footing, bringing this old devil down on me." He smiled again. "I'm sure it's nobbut a strain and bruising. If you get this off me, I'll be up and limping around in no time."

Callum wrapped his arms around the trunk and tried to heave it off Rory's leg. Despite his best effort, he was able to move it only slightly. Rory's groan pierced Callum when he had to lower the trunk again.

Rory's face was gray, and sweat stood out on his forehead. His eyes were closed and he said nothing when Callum said, "It's no use. I'm not strong enough. I'll have to use the oxen."

It seemed to Callum that his fingers and thumbs had swollen to twice their normal size, so clumsy were they unbuckling the oxen's harness to free them from the wagon. "Come on," Callum cried, holding the harness and trying to pull them over to where Rory lay. The oxen did not move. One even began to crop the grass. Callum yelled again, shrillness invading his voice. He glanced over his shoulder, hoping Rory might offer some solution, but he remained locked in a private world of pain.

Finally, Callum remembered that Rory got the stubborn beasts to move by clicking his tongue at them. Despite the sudden dryness of his mouth, Callum managed a passable click or two, but to no avail. Callum felt sobs starting to build deep in his chest, and he did his best to fight them down. Now he noticed that Dog was behind the oxen. "No, Dog!" he shouted, happy to be able to vent his frustration and fear. "You'll only fright them. Move away!"

Dog ignored Callum and made a series of small rushes forward, nipping at the hooves of the oxen. The two massive beasts leaped forward as if they had been goaded, and Callum guided them the way he wanted them to go. With their eyes rolling and heads tossing, the oxen looked ready to bolt, but Callum kept a tight grip on their harness and finally had them standing in front of the fallen trunk.

"Dog, get round here." Callum's voice was strained and husky with unshed tears. Before he had time to explain what it was that he wanted, Dog stood by his side. She placed her front paws and legs flat on the ground, her rump in the air, fixing the oxen with a baleful stare that froze them to the spot. Callum wrapped the rope around the tree trunk, then tied it to the oxen's harness, muttering to himself, "Please, God, let this work. Let the knots hold."

He gave the nearest ox a hard thwack on its solid hindquarter. With a high yodeling bark, Dog moved backward and the oxen advanced, dragging the tree with them.

Callum tried to drive the oxen so that the trunk would be dragged clear of the road, but a deep moan of pain from Rory stopped him. He lay with his eyes closed and teeth clenched.

Callum gasped when he saw Rory's leg. Bright blood ran freely from a deep gash. Fighting a faintness that threatened to overwhelm him, Callum forced himself to move closer and kneel down. Reaching out with a trembling hand, he gently touched his uncle's leg, causing Rory to wince with pain. Callum saw a flash of bone in the wound and heard a grating sound. "Uncle?" Callum sounded reedy, the voice of a scared little boy. "What should I do? It's no just a strain." He could not hold back a sob and, shamed, he turned away.

It seemed minutes before Rory answered. He struggled to a sitting position, although the effort obviously cost him dearly. When he caught his breath, opened his eyes and looked at the ruin of his leg, all color left his face.

Dog whined.

The noise seemed to bring Rory back to himself and he spoke. "Dinna panic, Callum, lad. Get two branches, good, long, straight ones, and strap them to my leg."

Relieved that Rory was once more in charge, Callum set to, concentrating on the search for suitable branches. When he found them, he stood puzzled, unable to think how to secure them.

"You're doing fine, laddie." Callum winced to hear how hoarse and weary Rory sounded. "Use my scarf and yours for bindings."

As Callum worked, he was conscious of how each movement hurt Rory, and he struggled to be both fast and gentle. By the time he had the makeshift splint in place, Rory's eyes were closed once more.

Dog barked. Standing in front of the oxen, she had them boxed in between the road and trees. The trunk was no longer on the road. With a sigh of relief, Callum now knew what his next task should be. Freeing the ropes from the trunk, he drove the oxen back, with Dog's help, to the wagon, harnessing them as quickly as he could.

Leaving Dog to ensure that the oxen did not bolt, Callum knelt beside Rory and placed Rory's arm around his shoulders. "Uncle, I'm going to try and get you into the wagon, but you're going to have to help me. I'll no be able to lift you."

Rory nodded and, as Callum struggled to his feet, he pushed with his good leg. Rory's weight was such that they nearly overbalanced. Rory did not speak, but small groans escaped between lips pressed together so tightly that they were but a thin white line in the red of his beard. Hopping, using Callum as a crutch, Rory made his painful way to the back of the wagon and fell forward so his upper body rested on its bed. "I cannae climb. Callum, you'll have to boost me."

Callum placed his hands on his uncle's waist and pushed.

Scrabbling with his hands for purchase, Rory worked his way into the wagon. Once there, he didn't move. Dog jumped up and lay alongside him. One of Rory's hands snaked out, feeling blindly until it came to rest upon Dog's shoulder.

Callum stood, staring, until a low growl from Dog freed him and suddenly he couldn't move fast enough. He ran to the wagon and leaped onto the seat when a harsh sound stopped him dead.

"Not home, laddie." Rory spoke with an urgency and strength that surprised Callum. "Take me to Josh Mason's place. I dinna want to fright Trude and the bairns."

Such was Rory's vehemence that Callum did not argue. Fortunately, the wagon and oxen were facing toward the village, and a click from Callum soon had them plodding steadily down the road. Callum had never driven the oxen on such a long journey. He tensed at every imagined slowing down, but they moved steadily and soon they were through the village and out into the countryside. Callum kept glancing around. Rory lay unmoving, his eyes closed, grimaces of pain contorting his face when the wagon hit a pothole or swerved to avoid a stump. Dog remained motionless by his side, scanning the road ahead.

Suddenly, Callum panicked — never having been to the Masons' farm, he had no idea where to go. Desperately he searched the trees on either side for an opening, but saw nothing. He was about to give up and ask Rory for help when Dog rose to her feet and began to bark, staring fixedly at the right-hand side of the road. Callum saw that there was indeed a small track.

"Is this it, Dog? How in hell do you know that?" Callum pulled on the reins, breathing a sigh of relief when the oxen turned and moved into the opening. Brush and branches overhung it, whipping Callum's face. "You'd think with so many hands to work, Mason would do a better job than this keeping it clear," he grumbled. The farther they got into the wood, the wider and clearer the track became, and it was with huge relief that Callum saw a clearing in which stood a large sturdy cabin, so big it was almost a house. In front of it, sitting on a stump and sharpening an ax was

Josh Mason. Amy, with the two smallest boys in tow, was working in the vegetable garden.

Before Callum had time to call out, Mason spotted the wagon. "Callum Murdoch, is it not? By', you're quite the man now, aren't you, driving the wagon by yourself. Has Big Rory sent you over for something or are you just taking the air?" Mason's laughter stopped when he saw how white Callum's face was. Dropping his ax, he ran as fast as he could toward them.

As Mason drew near, a muddle of words poured out of Callum.

Mason went straight to the wagon and looked down at Rory, who appeared to be sunk in a faint. "A lightning-struck tree, you say?"

Callum closed his eyes in relief — he was making some sort of sense. "Aye." Fear welled up inside him as he finally said what he had known ever since he lifted the trunk, "The leg is broken. We splinted it as best we could. Uncle Rory said to come here." All his fears came bursting out, "I didnae know what to do. There was blood, and I saw the bone. He's going to be all right, isn't he? You can do something, can't you?"

Mason put his hand on Callum's shoulder. "We'll do our best, my boy. Drive the wagon close to the house." He looked round. "Amy, get a bed ready!" he shouted. "Big Rory's been hurt." He pointed at one of the little boys. "Elijah, find the others. I need them here."

After that, it seemed to Callum that only minutes passed before Rory was resting on what was obviously Mason's own bed. His eldest son, Hosea, had been dispatched to Ancaster to fetch the American doctor who had recently settled there. Another son, Amos, fed and watered the oxen and then, tying a mule to the back of the wagon, set off to return the team to Trude and the children and let them know what had befallen Rory and Callum.

Apart from helping Mason and his sons lift the unconscious bulk of Rory from the wagon and into the house, Callum felt useless. He retreated to the fireplace, hunkering down on a stool, and was soon lost in thought. *If only*, hammered in his head. He saw himself taking his ease by the creek while Rory lay in pain. The great gash in Rory's leg he was sure had come about because he was so cack-handed in removing the tree. He forced back his sobs, but could not stop the tears that silently ran down his cheeks. Dog, who had remained close by Rory, padded over and licked the tears from one cheek. A small whine escaped her and she sat by Callum's side, resting her head companionably on his knee. He stroked her head and the thick ruff of fur behind it.

Amy Mason found them like that when she came to stir a pot of stew bubbling on the cooking trivet. "Callum, don't cry," she said. "Rory will be all right, you'll see. Pa will sort everything out."

Amy's kind words were the last straw. Callum sobbed and blurted out, "It's all my fault, I know it!"

"No." Amy put her arms around Callum and he leaned into her embrace. "Accidents like this are commonplace. All settlers fear them, but they can't avoid them. Why, Pa broke his arm last year logging and, see, he's as right as rain now."

A sound from the bed caused both Amy and Callum to jump up. Rory had come round and, although his face was still white with pain, he spoke clearly. "Ah, Callum laddie, you made it." He pulled a face. "Every jolt in that wagon sent knives into my leg. More than I could bear, it was." A furrow appeared between his eyes. "Trude," he said. "Has anyone told her?"

"Pa sent Amos over," Amy said, as the door flew open. Josh Mason and Hosea shepherded in the doctor, who was all business, immediately calling for hot water to wash his hands before he examined his patient.

Tall and clean shaven, the doctor was dressed in black, a huge, angular crow. His large hands were gentle as he untied the splint and cut away Rory's britches to get a better look at his leg.

"Hmm," he said. "The break itself is clean. Splinting it straight away has helped, but I've no liking for the look of this gash. Something jagged caused it and there's dirt in the wound."

Guilt once again washed over Callum. "It was a branch, I think, sir, when I pulled the tree trunk clear of my uncle's leg."

The doctor paid no attention. "Mr. Mason, do you have any alcohol?"

Mason nodded, and Amy fetched a quart earthenware jug. The doctor opened it, sniffed and took a hearty swig.

"Ah!" he said, smacking his lips, "a fine whisky." He gestured to Callum and Mason. "Raise him up."

They struggled to get Rory into a sitting position, and the doctor handed him the whisky. "Take a couple swallows. This is not going to be pleasant."

Rory did as he was told. He closed his eyes and waited. Barely a moan escaped him as the doctor pulled his leg straight and strapped it tightly into the splint once more. He roared out loud though when the doctor liberally splashed whisky into the gash, wiping it with a clean cloth before bandaging it. Through gritted teeth, Rory said, "By God, that's a waste of good whisky!"

A grim smile appeared on the doctor's face. "We'll see if it's a waste," he said. "There's some say that it prevents infection. Let's hope they're right. You're to rest, man. I'll swing by and see you in a week or so. I have to pass by here on my way to the village."

"I don't live here," Rory blurted out. "My farm's on the other side of the village."

The doctor looked hard at him. "It's no good to your leg to be moved. I'd advise biding where you are." Seeing how stricken Rory looked, he added, "At least until I've had another look at you."

"No!" Rory was determined. "I've a wife and bairns who need me. I'm going home."

The doctor started to speak, but Josh Mason interrupted. "You don't know MacBean, sir. He's the most stubborn man in the valley. No matter what you tell him, he'll do as he pleases." He laughed. "Why, I wouldn't put it past him to try and walk home!"

The doctor leaned over Rory. "Do ye hear me, man?" he bellowed. "You'll be no damn use to your wife and little ones a cripple, will you? Or worse still, dead from an infection."

Rory sank back onto the pillows, his distress evident in the sadness engraved on his face. "I hear what you're saying, but how can I rest easy here, not knowing how they are faring and with winter coming on?" His voice sank as he pleaded, "Let me get home and I'll swear not to walk until you say so." When the doctor hesitated, he added, "On my honor, sir!"

"I see that you'll not hear sense. At least get one night's good rest here to set you up. I'll leave some laudanum for the pain." Raising a hand, he waved away Rory's protests. "I know, I know, you can bear it, but we'll see what you say when you've been jolted to hell and back getting home. I'll get directions to your farm and be out in a week. If you need me before then, send for me." With that, he turned, took Josh Mason by the shoulder and led him to the doorway, where they stood deep in conversation for several minutes.

Callum moved closer to the bed now that there was space. Dog followed him and rested her head there so that she could lick Rory's hand, lying limp on the covers.

"Uncle, I'm so sorry!" Callum's words were hard to hear, choked as they were by tears.

"Ach, laddie, what have you got to be sorry for? If it wasnae for you, I'd still be lying there."

Callum looked down at Dog and stroked her head. "It was Dog that did it," he muttered, but Rory was asleep.

Amy gently took Callum's arm. "Let him sleep now. He's right, you know, you did well." She indicated a chair at the table. "Sit down and I'll bring you food. You can bunk in with Hosea and Amos tonight. Tomorrow, Pa will sort things out, don't you worry."

Callum sat with his head in his hands. Dog sat beside him, but he took no notice of her whines or nudges. He was lost in a whirlpool of guilt and shame. He ate mechanically when Amy gave him a bowl of stew and made no protest when she led him to a lean-to off the main house where Mason's older sons slept. He craved the black oblivion of sleep — and welcomed it when it came.

> > >

Callum was surprised to find that he had slept deeply, not even waking when the Mason boys came to bed. The morning was crisp and clear. Rory too had slept, although it was evident from his face that he was in pain. He greeted Callum warmly, praising him for his level-headedness, which made Callum want to run from the house and lose himself in the woods once more.

Josh Mason was all business. He had made a makeshift pallet in the bed of his wagon, using pillows and rolled-up blankets to try to ensure that Rory would experience as little movement as possible. He insisted that Rory take some drops of laudanum in water. With ill grace, Rory complied only when Mason told him they would not set out unless he did. It took Mason, his three eldest sons and Callum to lift Rory and carry him to the wagon. Once he was settled, Dog jumped up and lay beside him. Josh Mason motioned to Callum to sit on the driver's bench.

Mason drove slowly and carefully, skillfully directing the oxen to avoid nearly all the jolts in the road. At first, he kept glancing back at Rory, but when the laudanum claimed him and he sank into a deep sleep, Mason turned to Callum.

"You heard the doctor, Callum. Rory's not to use that leg at all."

"Aye." Callum wondered why Mason was reminding him. Surely his aunt was the one who needed to be told.

Mason took his eyes from the road briefly and looked hard at Callum. "Yesterday you proved yourself a steady boy and that's good, because a lot of extra work is going to fall on your shoulders now."

Callum was surprised to feel Dog's nose press into his back. "But I'll not be there, Mr. Mason," Callum said. "You've not forgotten that I am to start schoolmastering next week."

"That'll have to wait. Your aunt will have great need of you. You'll have to take Rory's place."

A vast surge of disappointment raced through Callum, but he made no sound save a squeal of pain as Dog's teeth nipped the tender flesh of his neck.

Chapter Nine

Muttering, Callum trudged wearily along the track through the woods. The light covering of snow made it easier to drag the sled on which lay the carcass of a small deer, but Callum cursed the coldness that had invaded the very marrow of his bones.

He had been out for hours before he spotted the two deer, hungrily nibbling the bark of a tree. Nothing had been said, but Callum had seen the look of relief on his Aunt Trude's face when he told her he intended to hunt that day. Everyone was sick of salted pork. In the four weeks since Rory's accident, fresh meat had been a rare treat. Once Rory had recovered from the fever that had swallowed the first week whole, he had shown Callum how to construct snares for rabbits, but no matter where Callum placed them, he had yet to catch one. Dog had been the family's mainstay, catching rabbits and hares, but, with seven mouths to feed, they did not go far. Callum knew he had to succeed. Trude worried that soon their salted pork would run out, and it had to see them through to spring.

A hidden root caused Callum to stumble, and it was only by steadying himself on Dog's strong back that he remained upright. "Damn it all to hell!" he cursed, kicking the root. When Dog turned her soft gaze upon him, he said, "And you can keep your understanding looks to yourself. You have no idea how much I hate this!"

Dog whined as if in disagreement, but Callum continued to rant and rail, savoring the feel of his rage. "Day after day! Feed and water the animals. Chop wood for the fire. Fetch water." He stopped, pulled off his mitten and looked at his hand. "Look at this!" he said, waving it in front of Dog's muzzle. "Look at those calluses. I've become a laboring man, the one thing my father feared, the thing he worked so hard all his life to escape. Oh, I know it's different here, Dog, but soon all I'll be fit for is manual work, no more copperplate for me."

Callum's expression became dreamy. "Just think, if Uncle Rory had not had his accident, I'd be in town now, in a warm classroom, discussing poetry." Dog snorted, but Callum took no notice. "Mebbe it can still happen. I mean, it's almost a month now; perhaps Uncle Rory could get about with a stick. If Sandy took over the wood chopping and the animals."

Dog positioned herself directly in front of Callum, bared her teeth and growled, her eyes boring into him.

He looked away. "Ach, you're right, Dog. The doctor said he was to stay off that leg for at least six weeks." The growling stopped and Dog relaxed, moving forward to lick Callum's bare hand. "I know, I know, I'm being selfish," he said. A grimace twisted Callum's features. "If I hadnae taken so long on that errand, mebbe he wouldnae have got hurt." Callum sighed. "But the work never changes. It's so dull." He shuddered. "Sometimes, at night, when I can't sleep, I get to thinking and worrying. What if the weather sets in and no one can get to town? I'd have to wait a whole year before I can begin the school." A smile suddenly brightened Callum's face. "But, Dog, with the doctor coming today, we'll have some new books to read. Uncle said he was going to lend us some poetry books. Let's hurry back. We might see him." His grin grew broader. "He likes an argument, does the doctor, and Uncle Rory's more than a match for him. It makes for fine entertainment to hear the two of them go at each other — a stubborn Scot and a damn Yankee!"

Callum's feet fairly flew, and he soon reached the clearing where the cabin stood. Leaving the sled with its bloody burden outside with Dog standing guard against wild animals, he burst into the cabin.

Rory looked up from his chair by the fire. "Well, laddie?" he asked. "Is it a successful hunter you've been?"

"Have I missed him? Has he been?" Callum scanned the cabin for some sign that they had had a visitor. He spotted a pile of books at the side of Rory's chair and didn't know whether to rejoice or cry.

"I'm afraid you have, Callum." Trude's voice was gentle. "He asked after you and said that you should be sure to let him know what you think of a book he brought specially for you, some poems by a Scots man, a Mr. Burns." Looking up from her sewing, Trude saw the disappointment etched on Callum's face and added, "He waited on you, but the weather's showing signs of turning and he wanted to get back to Ancaster before night fell."

Callum managed a smile. "Next time." Sensing his uncle's questioning gaze, he gestured in what he hoped was a casual manner toward the door. "I shot a deer."

Rory's face exploded into a smile and he almost leaped to his feet, remembering only at the last minute that he was not yet allowed to put weight on his bad leg. He hopped awkwardly, trying to keep his balance before falling back into the chair. "Well done, laddie!"

Trude ran over to Callum and hugged him and kissed him. Callum blushed, but did not turn away.

"Roast venison tonight and the rest I can smoke or dry." Little Jamie, puzzled by the adults' excitement, left off chasing a ball and tottered over. Trude picked him up and swung him round. "And you shall have a fine bone to chew on, little mannie, help those teeth of yours."

Rory was reaching for the crude crutches that he and Callum had fashioned. "Trude, help me into my coat and boots and get me outside."

"But, Rory —" she protested.

"No buts, my dear. I'll be careful. Callum and Sandy can drag my chair out for me. We need to butcher the deer quickly, and Callum hasnae done this before."

And so it was. Rory sat like a king giving orders. Sandy and Callum worked hard, following Rory's instructions as best they could. Callum hated the stench of blood and kept fighting down an urge to vomit, but he got the job done by thinking of how good the meat would taste when roasted — and of the books that awaited him. A small flame of pride kept him going, too. Here he was, keeping the family going, the family that had so readily taken him in as one of their own.

All the while, Dog sat watching, thick ropes of drool hanging from her jowls, until Rory took pity on her. The first thing the two boys had done was to gut the deer, pulling out its internal organs. Despite Rory's instructions to handle the liver carefully, Sandy had dropped it and then, in his haste to retrieve it, had stepped on it. It was a sorry sight, covered in dirt and flattened. Pointing at it with the end of a crutch, Rory said, "Throw that to Dog." At Sandy's questioning look, he added, "I know it's the bit your mother says is best, but she would fuss about the state it's in, whereas Dog willnae mind." When Sandy still hesitated, Rory said with mock ferocity, "And who, Master Alexander MacBean, has kept meat in your ever-hungry belly the last month or so?"

Dog yipped as if pleased with this logic and jumped up, her tail wagging. Sandy carried the meat over to her and, although the drool came even faster, she did not snatch the delicacy from him, but took it gently. After that, hunger overcame her good manners and she wolfed down the liver in great gobbling bites.

The afternoon light was dim by the time the butchering was done. Callum and Sandy were both spattered with blood. They helped Rory in and then carried in the meat. Trude already had a haunch of venison roasting, and its savory smell filled the cabin. While Callum and Sandy had been working, she had prepared a half barrel full of brine and molasses, and she dropped the three remaining leg joints into the mixture to soak before she smoked them. "You've done well, boys," she said and kissed them both.

Rory, full of pride, added, "And did ye know, woman, that yon city boy is a bit of a hawkeye. One shot was all he needed!"

Even Sandy looked awed and Callum felt a surge of pleasure. Grinning broadly, he said, "Our work's not done, yet, Uncle. We've still the animals to feed and water. Let's do that now, Sandy, and then we'll clean ourselves up and partake of this fine supper."

Dog nuzzled Callum's hand, as he set off outside once more, a spring in his step.

A harsh wind had blown up and Callum pulled his coat tighter around his bony frame. "Where did this come from?" he asked no one in particular. Dog whined and pressed close against his leg.

Coming up behind him, Sandy peered into the gloom. "The doctor's right. There's a snowstorm coming."

"How can everyone be so sure?" Callum's puzzlement was evident in his voice.

"Look at the sky. It's got a grayish, yellowish tinge to it. That's a sure sign, and the wind's coming from the north."

As if to confirm Sandy's prediction, heavy flakes began to drift from the sky. Callum caught one on his hand and watched it melt, marveling at how fluffy it looked, but how cold it felt.

That evening passed quickly. Everyone ate their fill of the rich meat. Trude had even baked an apple pie, using some of the apple rings she had so carefully dried in the autumn. The doctor's books were a treasure trove. He had included a copy of *Gulliver's Travels*, and Rory enthralled the family with the adventures of Lemuel Gulliver amongst the tiny inhabitants of Lilliput. Callum took himself off to one side and, with Dog lying companionably next to him, lost himself in the poems of his countryman Mr. Robert Burns.

> > >

The next morning, Callum knew that something was different. Although the cabin windows were small, their oiled-paper coverings usually let in at least a little light, but today there seemed to be none. Trude, already preparing breakfast, had as many rushlights burning as she would at night. The wind howled around the cabin, seeming intent on finding its way in through any chink it could find. Callum, Dog at his heels, ran to the cabin door and was about to fling it open when Rory's shout stopped him.

"Callum, get your coat, boots, scarf and gloves and wait for Sandy before you venture out. There are all the signs of a heavy snowfall." Before Callum could protest that Scotland had occasional snow, his uncle continued, "If it's as deep as I think it is and it shows no sign of letting up, mebbe it's the time to set up the rope."

"The rope?"

Coming up behind him, Sandy laughed. "I'll get it, Dadda, and show him what to do. It's in case there is a blizzard, Callum, and we can't see our way to the barn!"

Callum's face showed his disbelief that such a thing would ever be needed, but he was glad he had said nothing when he opened the door.

A wall of snow, as high as his waist, barricaded them in the cabin. Great gusts of wind drove the snow into his face and Callum stepped back, almost tripping over Dog.

"Get the spades and start digging. We need to get the door shut as quickly as we can. As soon as you're outside, tie the rope to the cabin. Wind it round your waist, Callum. That way it'll not be tangling your feet and you'll have it with you by the time you make it to the barn." Rory rattled off more orders, then ruefully added, "It's hard work, I know, boys, and I wish I could be doing it for you. Be as quick as you can, for even from here I can feel the fierceness of the cold."

The snow was heavy, but Sandy and Callum worked quickly, mindful of Rory's words. Once they'd cleared a circle big enough for them and Dog to stand in, Callum had his first real chance to look at what the storm had brought — and was still bringing.

The familiar terrain of Trude's garden and the clearing had been completely obliterated. In the clouds of white, Callum could make out bumps and hillocks where the snow had drifted. The barn was merely a dark shape whose outlines were blurred and softened so that it took on an unreal aspect.

Dog barked and Callum realized that Sandy was urging him to start digging again before they all froze in place. He set to and soon lost himself in the rhythm of bending, scooping and flinging the snow as they forged toward the barn. It was hard work, which would normally raise a sweat in minutes, but the biting wind put paid to that, and Callum felt his fingers and toes slowly becoming numb. This was like no winter he'd ever seen in Scotland. He could hear Sandy grunting with exertion beside him, and a wave of pity for the boy swept through him — and a realization of how hard Sandy worked and how little he complained.

Dog suddenly pushed between the two boys and barked furiously.

"Whisht your row!" Callum said. "Don't we have it hard enough without you playing games?"

It was only when Callum looked up, which he had avoided doing to save his eyes from the stinging snow, that he saw what concerned Dog. In their blind hurry, they had not dug straight and, if they continued on their present path, they would have dug a path to the side of the barn rather than the front. Callum ruffled the snow-covered fur on Dog's head. "A proper guardian angel, aren't you, girl?" he said. Then it struck him how easy it would be to lose one's way when battered by the wind and snow.

"Come on, Sandy!" he yelled with a wry grin. "Dog is keeping us on the straight and narrow."

With Dog as their eyes, the barn was soon reached. Even over the howling wind, the bass bellowing of the oxen and the plaintive lowing of the cow could be heard. The animals liked the weather no more than Callum and Sandy did. So distressed were they that, for once, they made no protest when Dog entered the barn. Callum and Sandy quickly gave them fodder and broke the ice to get water from the barrel kept just inside the barn door. The cow's udder was distended and Callum milked her as fast as his frozen, clumsy fingers would allow. Both boys were shivering, longing to get back to the warmth of the cabin.

"Do you think we should clean out their stalls?" Sandy's face was gray, and he was hard-pressed to speak clearly, so badly were his teeth chattering.

"No, it'll no hurt to miss one day." Callum spoke with the certainty of his desire to be back by the fire reading. "Your dadda will understand."

"But —"

"Don't argue!" Callum's tone was harsh and Sandy flinched. "Come on, stop wasting time, you wee sucky babby!" Callum regretted the words as soon as he spoke and he felt worse when he saw tears well in Sandy's eyes. Callum made for the door, his head down, the bucket of milk banging annoyingly against his leg. He ignored Dog, who growled behind him and, when Sandy still hesitated, he used his free hand to grab him by the wrist and drag him toward the cabin, down the narrow path they had so painstakingly cleared.

The storm continued for the rest of the day. At times, the wind was so strong that Callum could have sworn the cabin moved on its foundation. He spent the day curled by the fire with a book as planned, but it was hard to concentrate, and enjoyment was strangely absent. The younger children were fractious and any game that Trude started with them soon ended in tears. Sandy whittled on a stick and glowered at Callum, obviously still angry. Rory kept asking either Callum or Sandy to crack open the door and see if the snow was still falling.

Even Dog was affected. She could not seem to find a comfortable place to lie and paced the cabin, whining. Every so often, she would go to the door and press her nose against it, sniffing, and then growl. Callum lost count of the times he told her to sit down. His patience snapped late in the afternoon.

The wind had died down a little, and the atmosphere in the cabin seemed to have lightened, too. Callum was finally lost in his book when Dog suddenly stiffened, the hair on her spine rose, and she howled, a long ululating howl that hung in the air.

"Good God, Dog, what's the matter now?" Callum got wearily to his feet and went to where Dog stood trembling by the door. "You cannae go out and that's an end to it, you stupid beast!"

Dog looked up at him with reproachful eyes, but she did not move, not even when Callum seized her by the scruff of the neck and attempted to pull her away from the door. In frustration, he shouted, "That's it, I've had enough! Go lie down by the fire and let's have an end to your disturbances." Dog dug her claws in and howled even louder.

"Callum, leave her be!" Rory's voice was angry. "There's something wrong." He cocked his head and listened.

A faint rhythmic banging could be heard above the wind.

Rory made as if to struggle from his seat, but Trude motioned him back and went to the door. Wrapping her shawl around her shoulders, she stepped outside. When she came back in, she looked scared. "It's the barn door. It's open and banging in the wind."

Callum felt fear clutch him. All he saw was his hurried departure from the barn that morning. Had he snagged the door shut? Before Sandy could say anything, he said, "I'll go and see what's amiss." Ignoring Rory's protests, which turned into instructions once he saw that Callum's mind was set, Callum wrapped himself up as warmly as he could, pulling Rory's fur hat over his head. Calling for Dog to accompany him, he ran outside.

It had snowed steadily all day, but the path he and Sandy had made was still passable. The temperature had fallen and the snow crunched and squeaked under his boots and Dog's paws. He heard rustling and turned to see Rory leaning on Trude silhouetted in the open doorway of the cabin. As quickly as he could, he trudged to the barn. The door had obviously been open for some time, because snow had drifted in. Peering into the dark interior, Callum made out the shape of the cow lying down in her byre, pressed up against the rough wooden wall. He turned — and froze — the oxen's stall was empty, its rails smashed and trampled.

Callum raced to the door, but he could not see any hoofprints. The oxen were long gone.

Rory's voice rang out, "Callum, laddie, what is it?"

Callum could hardly bring himself to tell his uncle the dreadful thing that had happened through his own carelessness. His voice cracking, he shouted, "It's the oxen. They've got out, but dinna worry. Dog and I will find them."

With Rory's groan of anguish in his ears, Callum set off blindly, determined to make this mishap good. He did not look back even when Rory called to him, "Callum, come back! Night's falling. You cannae go searching now."

Chapter Ten

Callum forced his way through the snow, oblivious to how deeply piled it was now that he had left the path between cabin and barn. The intense cold did not register. He was fired by shame that, once again, his carelessness threatened the family with ruin. *I didnae bolt the door. I didnae bolt the door*, pounded continually in his head. Dog ran alongside Callum, but he ignored her increasingly frantic barks and whines, until she suddenly veered and threw her full weight against his legs. Taken by surprise, he lost his balance and fell. From under his eyelids, tears oozed and froze on his cheeks.

Dog stepped closer and delicately licked a frozen tear away. Her breath steamed. Then she sat down and waited, her discomfort evident in the tenseness of her body.

Callum buried his face in her thick fur. Between sobs, he choked out his misery. "I cannae do anything right, Dog. I thought I'd got better.

Since Uncle Rory's been laid up, I have, I know I have. I've worked hard. But it's this land, there's always something new, some danger that waylays me. Always, always, I do something stupid. I just don't think, and then it's too late. The oxen ... what will we do if I can't find them? There's no way Uncle could buy new ones. Without them ..." The prospect of trying to carve out a farm without the brawn of the oxen was too horrible to contemplate.

Dog made a whiffling noise deep in her throat. Shaking her large head, she eased herself out of Callum's desperate embrace and rose to her feet. A sharp bark stopped Callum from subsiding into a heap of misery.

He looked at her and then looked around. He had come some distance into the woods. Snow came to Callum's knees, stretching ahead of him unmarked. "Och, Dog, do you not see it's hopeless? Those bluidy animals are long gone without a trace of their passing. I'll never find them." Callum put his head in his hands.

On stiff, determined legs, Dog advanced on Callum, taking the cloth of one sleeve firmly between her teeth. At first, her pulling met with resistance, but soon she had Callum back on his feet. Dog bounded forward, her deep chest plowing through the snow. She looked back at Callum. When he made no move, she let loose a volley of loud, angry, insistent barks that did not let up until he spoke.

"What's the point, Dog? We have no way of knowing where they went. It's dark and I'm set to freeze here." Callum shivered as if realizing just how cold the night had become. He made as if to go back the way he had come, but Dog barked again.

With her nose down to the snow, Dog took a few more bounding steps, looked up to make sure Callum was watching then repeated her actions.

Clapping his hands against his sides, Callum laughed. "By God, is there no end to your talents, Dog? Are you telling me you can track them?"

Dog chuffed deep in her chest, her tail wagging, and set off once more. Callum followed her, hope rising. She moved purposefully, forcing her way through the snow like a ship breasting heavy seas. Her coat was frosted with the debris of her passing, and she seemed to glow in the moonlight. Dog stayed on the oxen's trail until they were deep in the woods.

Callum did his best to keep up, although he found the going increasingly hard despite Dog's breaking the trail for him. The effort of lifting his feet high enough to clear the snow caused his legs to ache. His breathing was becoming labored, and he felt as if he would never be warm again. He was grateful for Dr. Lennie's thick wool coat and the shawls, scarves and gloves that Aunt Trude had knitted for him. And for Rory's fox-fur hat;

although it had a tendency to fall down over his eyes, it did at least keep his ears warm.

"Dog. Dog!" Callum's voice was hoarse and strained. "Slow down. I cannae keep up this pace."

Dog looked back over her shoulder, but, if anything, her speed increased slightly, her indication that there was no time to waste.

Cursing under his breath, Callum realized that the gap between himself and Dog was widening. A fist of fear squeezed his heart at the thought that he might be left alone in this frozen wasteland. To add to his misery, snow started to fall once more and the wind rose. At first, the snow was light, a mere irritation, but it quickly thickened and Callum struggled to see more than a little ways ahead.

"Dog! Dog! Don't leave me!" Callum's high keening cry was whipped away by the wind. Relief flooded through him when a blocky, black shape came barreling back toward him. He reached down to grasp Dog's fur, intending to hold on, to use her strength like a walking stick, but she adroitly avoided his hand, turned and set off into the swirling snow once more, barking at regular intervals. Callum threw back his head and howled his despair.

The barking drilled into Callum's ears until he wanted to scream. Then, what Dog was doing suddenly hit him — barking was her way of guiding him. As long as he could hear her, he knew he was heading the right way, even though the visibility was worsening by the minute. With new strength and determination, Callum set off.

Dog led Callum on a twisting path through the trees. Small signs — a broken branch or torn bark — indicated that some large animal had passed this way, so Callum was sure that Dog knew what she was doing. He wondered at how far they had traveled, and what had caused the oxen to flee. As the storm strengthened, such thoughts became luxuries. The wind blasted snow into his face, and he walked doubled over to avoid its sting and, on occasion, to remain upright.

Dog's barking became more insistent, even panicky. For a moment, there was silence. Then she began to howl. Callum floundered forward as fast as he could, stumbling, clawing the snow, anything that would get him to Dog.

By the time Callum could see Dog, his heart was racing. She was alone. There was no sign of the oxen. He was so short of breath that he could not even call out to her. She was standing in a clear space, as if on guard. The snow had drifted to one side, forming a huge bank out of which trees protruded. With the ground relatively clear, Callum suddenly found himself able to run toward Dog.

Too late, Callum realized that Dog stood on the edge of a small drop. He was unable to stop himself and went tumbling over its edge. As he fell, a whirl of images assailed him — the flash of Dog's eyes and teeth as she lunged for him in a vain attempt to halt his fall; the brown shapes of the oxen, huddled together at the bottom of the drop; the lacelike patterns of snowflakes; a rock whose crest stuck out from the snow like a fang.

➤   ➤   ➤

Callum groaned. He tried to open his eyes and then wished that he had not. Everything was wavery and distorted, and he thought that his head must explode with the pain. He sensed something near him.

"Dog, is that you?" The words cost Callum dearly. A wave of sickness washed through him. He felt the world recede and then return. Coarse fur brushed against his cheek and he leaned into it, but Dog seemed intent on some task that he could only guess at, and she paid him no heed. He felt a tugging at his coat pocket. He struggled to work out what Dog was doing, but his concentration weakened. When he next forced his eyes open, an unbelievable sight was before him.

Snow was falling so fast and hard that it was like looking through tattered white curtains blowing in the wind. A tall, strongly built girl, her body cloaked by cascading dark hair, was standing with her back to him, looking at the oxen, who were tossing their heads, pawing the ground, rolling their eyes as if ready to bolt at any second. The girl spoke to them in a language unfamiliar to Callum, and this seemed to calm them, but their distress was still evident. She stamped one bare foot at them, but the oxen remained immobile.

Callum tried to sit up. Pain burned through one wrist when he put his weight upon it. He cried out and the girl turned and looked at him, her mouth drawn into a grimace of anguish. She made a sinuous gesture with her fingers. Callum felt darkness reach into him and swallow him up.

Hot breath on Callum's cheek roused him. He forced his eyes open once more and found himself staring into Dog's deep brown ones. "Was there a girl?" he whispered. "I saw her. Where has she gone, Dog? We must find her. We cannae leave her lost out here."

Dog whined and pushed at Callum with her nose.

Although his vision was still fuzzy, the dizziness was gone. Callum struggled into a sitting position, careful to favor his injured wrist. His hand hit something hard and smooth. It was Dog's box, which must have dropped from his pocket when he fell. Its carved top had cracked open. Alongside the box lay something gauzelike and shimmery that teased and tricked the eye into looking away from it. Instinctively, Callum scooped it up, ignoring Dog when she tried to push his hand away, and placed both it and the box safely in his pocket.

Dog whimpered.

Shivering, Dog pulled at Callum's coat until he was forced to his knees. He tried to stand, but the world began to spin and he retched, vomiting up all he had eaten that day. Stepping back, her muzzle wrinkled in distaste, Dog watched Callum. When she was sure he would vomit no more, she resumed pulling on his clothes, forcing him to move, crawling painfully on his hands and knees, until he was alongside one of the oxen. She worried at him until he finally managed to stand. When Callum swayed, Dog leaned against him so that he fell toward the ox. To save himself from falling headlong, Callum threw one arm around the ox's neck and rested his head against its smooth side, thankful for the support. Dog moved around behind the oxen and, just as she did after Rory's accident, forced them into motion by nipping lunges at their heels.

Callum was so cold that his body was racked by shivers. His aching head and wrist were jarred by each dragging step. Snow flew into his face so thickly that he felt in danger of being suffocated. Once Dog had got the oxen moving, they trudged at a steady pace, but the route they were forced to take was a roundabout one, as they could not climb the drop. There was a muzziness to Callum's thinking. The girl he had seen — or thought he saw — bothered him. There was something familiar about her. Was she a ghost? A phantom conjured up by his fall? If she was neither, what was she? What was she doing naked in the middle of a snowstorm? Where had she gone? Callum tried calling to Dog, but she remained intent on her herding.

Oh, but his head ached. Indeed it seemed as if his entire body was one big bruise, but his spirits lifted when he squinted against the driving snow and saw that they had reached the creek, but ten minutes from the cabin. Renewed strength coursed through him, along with a feeling of pride. He had found the oxen, and the farm was saved. A yelp from Dog brought him up short. She was right. He could take no credit for retrieving the oxen. Dog had done it. She had tracked them and brought them home, almost in spite of him. Without Dog, his misguided attempt to put right his mistake could so easily have ended in disaster, even death. Without Dog, he did not know how he would cope with this strange new life.

In the moonlight, Dog's eyes shone green, staring back at Callum until he was forced to drop his gaze. Then she shook herself, as if she was coming out of water. Snow spun from her coat, shining in the moonlight like flecks of silver fire. A quick nip on the heel caused the nearest ox to leap forward, and the animals picked up the pace, as if they, too, knew that home was nearby.

When they came into the clearing, the oxen broke into a trot and Callum released his grip. A deep ringing bellow echoed and bounced off the snow. The cabin door flew open and Rory, precariously balanced on a crutch, and Trude stood there.

"Callum, thank God! Running off into the night like that. We've been feared we'd lost you." Rory's shout almost equaled the power of the ox's bellow. He started forward, but Trude restrained him.

"Sandy," Trude called, "get the oxen safe in their stalls. Callum and Dog, get yourselves inside this instant. You'll be frozen, the both of you."

Squeezing past his parents, Sandy was already wrapped and bundled against the cold. The oxen were huddled by the barn and once Sandy threw open the door, they jostled each other in their eagerness to get into the relative warmth and comfort of their stall.

Callum found that, even without the support of the ox, he was surprisingly steady on his feet now. He looked round for Dog and saw her at the edge of the clearing, staring into the woods, so still that she could have been carved of black marble. Callum called, but she did not move. He limped over to her and knelt to place an arm around her shoulders. When she felt his touch, she turned her head toward him, once again silvery trails of tears ran down each side of her muzzle.

"Whisht, Dog, it's over. You saved the oxen and you saved me. I owe you so much." He stroked the tears away with a gentle hand. "Come in now, and warm yourself by the fire. I'll wager Aunt Trude will have some tasty treat for you when she hears what you did."

Dog stared into the snow a little longer, before following Callum slowly to the cabin.

Trude had got Rory ensconced once more in his chair by the fire. A bowl of hot water and a mug of sassafras steamed on the table. The three small children were peering from the cozy nests of their beds like little mice, their eyes big and wondering. Rory started to talk, but Trude said, "No, Rory, there'll be no questions or answers until these two are warm. Everyone is safe, that's what matters. The whys and wherefores can wait." She grabbed Callum and stripped him of his outer garments before wrapping him in a blanket and making him sit down to drink the tea. Her gentle fingers probed and cleaned the cut on his head. Trude sucked in her breath and said, "It's quite the goose egg you have, Callum, but nothing's broken. That you got yourself back tells me that the hard MacBean head has come into its own once more." She threw a teasing look at Rory. Having satisfied herself that Callum was comfortable, Trude beckoned Dog and made her stand by the bowl of water. Wetting a rag in the warm water, she carefully pulled away the lumps of snow that had collected on her fur like bunches of white grapes. When all was done, she gave Dog a slap on her rump. "Now, Dog, you go rest yourself by the fire. I've saved a bone for you." She rocked back on her heels, "Callum, if you've warmed up, your uncle is bursting with questions."

Rory's words poured out — anger at Callum's pig-headedness but relief that he had found the oxen and brought everyone back safely. At several points in his tirade, there were tears in his eyes, but he quickly knuckled them away.

Callum let the words wash over him, lending only half an ear. He was worried about Dog, who lay in a morose heap by the fire, her head resting on her paws, the bone untouched.

"So, now that we're agreed that you're a foolish young larrikin, how did you manage to wriggle out of what promised to be a disaster?" Rory launched into another recitation of all the dangers Callum had faced by rushing off into the night.

"It was Dog." Callum's simple declaration stopped Rory in mid-rant. "She found the oxen, and when I fell down the ravine ..."

"The ravine? Just how far did you fall?" Trude leaped to her feet in concern.

"I don't know, but it's nothing, just the bump on my head that you've already seen, and I think I've wrenched my wrist." Callum wanted to avoid further fussing.

Luckily, Rory was on his side. "Let the boy be, Trude. I want to hear what miracles this animal has performed now."

"When I fell, she watched over me until I came to, and then got me and the oxen home." Callum paused. "There was something strange though."

He stopped suddenly, realizing that he did not want to mention the girl he couldn't have seen, but was sure he had.

"Strange?" Rory's good humor was being restored. "Everything about that beast is strange." He laughed and Callum joined in, although his own laughter was forced. He was happy just to have the subject changed.

Trude took the break in the conversation to pack Callum off to bed, with instructions that he was to sleep as long as he liked. She and Sandy could cope without him for a day.

"My coat, where's my coat?"

Surprised by Callum's urgent tone, Trude gestured to where the coat lay, spread out on the settle to dry. Callum felt frantically in the pocket, sighing with relief when his fingers closed round the box and, next to it, the strange web. Clutching the coat to him, Callum wearily climbed the ladder to the loft.

Dog made no move to follow Callum.

Chapter Eleven

Callum awoke to the sound of voices from downstairs. His body ached a little, but he was surprised to find that he felt quite limber. He stretched his arms above his head until his joints cracked and yawned hugely. Remembering Trude's instructions to lie abed as long as he desired, he closed his eyes and fell back upon his straw tick, pulling the blankets up around his chin. He tried surrendering himself to a pleasant doze, but he could not. Something bothered him, but for the life of him, Callum could not pin it down. He reached out his hand for Dog, but his fingers encountered only bare boards. Callum sat bolt upright, frantically looking around. There was no sign of Dog. His heart beat fast in panic until he recalled her strange behavior of the previous night and her refusal to follow him to her usual resting place alongside his tick.

Callum spied a humped, black shape near his feet and, for one moment, thought Dog had crept into the loft after he was asleep. But he was looking at his coat, carelessly tossed when he fell into bed.

Callum pulled it toward him, thrust his hand deep into the pocket and pulled out Dog's box. In the dim light, he now saw that the carved top had been completely stoved in by his fall. The interior of the box was smooth and empty. What was it the man had said when he sold him Dog? "As long as you keep this box sealed like this, Bess is bound to be your true and faithful servant." Well, the box was certainly no longer sealed, but Dog had remained with Callum during the storm. Had the man been lying? Having witnessed his behavior and his cruel ways, that would have come as no surprise to Callum. He reached into his pocket again and pulled out the thing he had found alongside the box, the thing Dog had made a grab for.

It was like trying to hold a cobweb, crumpled and gauzy. Callum had trouble focusing on the thing; it seemed almost to be made of mist and shadows. By squinting fiercely, Callum was able to glean some sense of what it was. Although flimsy, it had a definite shape — a miniature human form. Worried that he might tear it, Callum pulled gently and was amazed by its elasticity and strength as it stretched effortlessly, until his arms were as far apart as they could go.

Whirling thoughts filled Callum's brain. The girl, the broken box, Dog's eldritch behavior, her un-doglike understanding, all were starting to make sense. Callum wondered whether a black, furry web of dark mist had lain on the ground beside him while the girl had stamped her feet at the stubborn oxen.

Callum started to sweat, a feeling of sickness rose and lodged in his throat. If what he thought was true, Dog could leave him unless he guarded what must obviously be her human form.

"No!" Callum's whisper was hoarse. "You can't. I need you." He crumpled up the web and thrust it back into the box, pressing down the broken wood despite the splinters that tore at his fingers. "I'll seal it so tight that no one will ever open it again." Callum stopped, stunned by the enormity of his thought. He would be keeping Dog captive, just as her previous owner had done. He couldn't do that. But he also couldn't imagine his life without Dog. He flung himself face down on the bed, the box clutched in his hand.

Then it came to him with blinding clarity. Dog wanted to stay. Hadn't she changed back of her own free will and come home, guiding Callum and the oxen to safety? She could have escaped there and then, leaving them to fend for themselves. Callum hastily pulled on his clothes. He went to the top of the ladder. At the bottom, looking up at him with her lambent eyes, was Dog.

When he reached the ground, Callum went to stroke Dog's head, but stayed his hand before it touched her. Somehow, it seemed wrong now. He shivered, pushing the troubling thought away. Everything was normal again. The oxen were safe. He and Dog were safe. Life would go on as before.

Dog butted her head at Callum's leg, more like a cat than a dog. He looked down at her and then wished he hadn't. He'd swear there was a beseeching in her eyes. In a voice that exuded a heartiness Callum did not feel, he said, "There, there, Dog. You're a fine animal, aren't you? Without you, none of us would have made it back." He knelt beside her and tousled her fur roughly, until she pulled away and flopped down by the fire with a sigh.

There was a different atmosphere in the cabin, and it took Callum a few seconds to realize why. The coverings on the windows glowed. The storm was over and the sun was out.

Rory spoke up from the fireside. "Aye, Callum, it's a fine day." He looked Callum over critically. "I'll wager, laddie, that you are a mass of aches and pains today."

"No, no, Uncle," Callum replied, going to the table where a breakfast of bread and jam was laid out for him. "My wrist pains me a little, but I'll be able to tend to the animals today."

"There's no need, Callum," Rory said. "Your aunt and Sandy are out there now. The two wee bairns have gone with them, but I'm sure they'll be frolicking in the snow and being more of a hindrance than a help. Wee Jamie's asleep in his crib, so there's time for you and me to talk."

Callum tore at the fresh bread with his teeth, surprised at how hungry he felt. He had been dreading this moment, knowing that Rory was going to lambast him for his carelessness. He said nothing, hoping only that the lecture would be brief.

"Callum, laddie," Rory spoke slowly, his voice gentle as he searched for the right words. "You do realize that you could have died out there last night, don't you? You cannae play fast and loose with the weather. Any settler who's worth his salt would have told you that the worst thing would be to go into the woods at night. It's so easy to get lost, and in the snow and with the wind howling." Rory stared at Callum, who looked down at his empty plate, licked his fingers and picked up the remaining crumbs. "Aye, Uncle, but," his voice was impassioned, "I had to make it right, see. My carelessness could have cost you all you've worked for!"

Rory struggled to his feet on his crutches and swung himself adroitly over to the table, dropping down onto the stump next to Callum. He put an arm around Callum's shoulders, drawing him to his chest, where he held him. "You've a good heart, Callum," Rory said, his words resonating through Callum, "but you're foolhardy." He sighed, releasing Callum from his bear hug and pushing him back to study his face. "What will I do with you?" he asked. "I don't think you grasp what danger you were in."

Callum answered, his eyes fixed unwaveringly on Dog's recumbent form by the fire. "I do, Uncle, honestly I do. But you forget that I have Dog. She saved my life last night —" he paused, "— and as long as she is with me, I'll not come to any harm."

Dog lifted her head and stared back at Callum.

➤ ➤ ➤

Days passed slowly in the snowbound cabin. Chores were done, books were read, and games were played. For the first time ever, Callum found a joy in his daily routine. He no longer found the work physically hard, tackling his chores with an ease he would have marveled at but a few months ago. Work had one other advantage: as long as he surrendered himself totally to it, he didn't have to think about Dog.

Rory's leg had strengthened enough to manage with only one crutch. He burned with impatience for the doctor to return, to give him the word as to when he might try to walk normally once again. Only the Christmas preparations distracted him, and he spent many hours carving by the fire when the little ones were outside or in bed.

Trude was knitting, but would not say for whom. Callum had no skills, save those of his pen and pencil, and he drew pictures of the cabin and the children, which he hoped would prove acceptable gifts. He was not used to gift giving. Christmas at home had been a contemplative time. His father spent much of the day in church, and the day was special only in the lavish meal Callum's mother served upon his father's return.

Dog was like a black cloud hanging over the preparations for the festivities. She spent so much of her time lying by the fire, staring into the flames, that Trude said she was more a hearth rug than a dog. Callum's smile in response was uneasy. He made a point of sitting near her when he drew, and she responded with a trace of affection, but the old camaraderie was gone. Only when playing with wee Jamie did Dog regain the joy and sweetness of spirit that Callum had come to love and now missed so much. He comforted himself with the thought that, once spring came and the two of them could roam freely, her spirits would be restored. He could not allow himself to think any differently, for when he did, guilt and sadness coursed through him, as if they would wash the very marrow from his bones.

The weather had continued fine, and when a warmer spell came, the snow started to melt. On Christmas morning, early, Sandy, who had been playing with a ball made from a pig's bladder, came tearing into the cabin, hollering, "Visitors! Visitors, we've got visitors!" His announcement had everyone in an uproar as they grabbed boots and shawls and piled out of the cabin to see who had come. By that time, Josh Mason was already helping Amy down from the wagon in the clearing. All his sons were with him and, much to Rory's delight, so was the doctor, astride his fine bay mare.

"Merry Christmas!" Rory's shout almost deafened Callum, on whom he leaned. "What a surprise!"

"We thought you would be starved of company, what with being laid up and with the snow," Mason replied. "The doctor said you were due a visit, and we suggested we make it a Christmas visit." He waved a hand toward Amy. "Amy has done us proud with her cooking and baking, so we've packed it up and brought it along so that we can have a feast." He laughed, pretending to pull a worried face. "That's if you'll have us."

Rory went as if to cuff Mason, almost overbalancing, and the merriment that this provoked in the younger children swept everyone else along. It was a laughing, rowdy party that wended its way into the cabin, packing it with bodies, until Callum was sure the walls would have to bend to accommodate them all.

The rest of the day was a happy one, one that Callum was sure he would recall when he was an old, old man. Trude and Amy did indeed produce a feast. The doctor examined Rory's leg, pronouncing it to be mending straight and true, and even allowing that he might just use a stick now as long as he promised to return to his usual chores only gradually. Many toasts were drunk to this decision before Rory raised his glass and said, "To yon bonny laddie, Callum, who has been —" here he paused, with a twinkle in his eyes, "— I was going to say my good right hand, but perhaps it should be my good right leg!"

Callum was surprised at the depth of emotion that Rory's words raised in him. He struggled with the words when he returned the toast. "To my new family and friends in Upper Canada, who have given me a home. To my new life here, whatever it may bring." He too hesitated and then said, "And to my dearest Dog."

Dog was wrestling with the smallest children, allowing them to wriggle and climb all over her. She stopped and let loose a small bark.

The visitors stayed until after lunch, timing their departure so that most of their journey would still be in daylight. Just before they left, Callum looked up from where he and Amy were entertaining the little ones with a game of knucklebones and realized that Rory, Trude, the doctor and Josh Mason were huddled together talking. Every so often they would glance in his direction. He strained to hear what they were saying, but the children were laughing and shouting in glee, and he could catch nothing.

After the excitement of the day, everyone was tired, and it was with dragging heels that Sandy and Callum readied themselves to bed down the animals for the night. Rory rose to his feet and, using the stick that he had insisted Josh Mason find for him before he left, made his way slowly to where his coat and hat hung by the door. "Sandy, my boy," he said expansively, "you are relieved of your duties tonight. I think it is time that I surveyed my domain." He laughed when he saw the look of puzzlement on Sandy's face. "We need to work on your vocabulary, young man. In plain English, you may have the night off. I'll help Callum."

Callum sensed how pleased Rory was to be able finally to return to some semblance of normalcy. He also wondered if his uncle had another motive, something to do with the conference among the grown-ups. As he muffled himself up, he called to Dog. "Are you coming, girl?" He winced at his thoughtless choice of words, a wince mirrored in the look of pain that passed over Dog's expressive face.

Dog padded slowly over to where Callum and Rory waited. Callum was surprised: of late, she had often been reluctant to leave the cabin.

The cow was lowing when they reached the barn, and Callum set to milking her straight away, enjoying the restful rhythm that he fell into. Rory went about giving the oxen fresh water, struggling with his stick and the bucket, making Callum realize that his help would be needed for quite a while yet. His sigh was echoed by Dog, lying in the doorway of the barn, gazing toward the woods.

Callum's reverie was interrupted by a tap on the shoulder. Rory awkwardly lowered himself onto a bale of straw, his bad leg stretched in front of him, so that he was level with Callum on the milking stool.

"Callum." Rory made sure that he had Callum's full attention by gently turning Callum's face to him. "I meant what I said this afternoon. We wouldnae have managed without you, the last wee while."

Callum was unable to prevent himself from saying, "If it hadnae been for my daydreaming, you'd no have got hurt, Uncle."

"Nay, laddie, you're being too hard on yourself." Rory's eyes were gentle. "What happened to me was an accident of my own making. I want to thank you for what you've done, all the more precious as farm work doesnae come natural to you." Here, Rory hesitated as he thought what to say next.

Callum blushed, not so much at the kindness of his uncle's words but more at the feeling that they were undeserved, for his uncle did not know how much he had resented what he had to do, and how he had cursed and groaned to Dog about it.

"You've changed." Rory grinned. "You're not a whey-faced city boy now, that's for sure." Becoming more solemn, he regarded Callum steadily. "But what you become is up to you now, and I know you'll make the right choices."

Callum watched in wonder as Rory carefully removed the thick gold earring he always wore and held it out to him. "Here, take this." Sensing Callum's confusion, Rory laughed. "It's a Highland custom, laddie. When a Highlander travels, especially on a long journey, his family gives him an earring so that should he die far frae home, amongst strangers, it'll provide for a decent burial." Rory's eyes grew misty. "Your mammie gave me this, Callum, when I left for the Americas, melted down what little jewelry she had. I've never taken it off my ear before, but it's time." Rory rubbed his eyes. "I'm home. I'll not be traveling anymore. But you, Callum, you've a long journey ahead." Rory took Callum's hand and closed it around the earring.

Callum had no words. He placed his free hand on top of Rory's and clasped it tightly.

"Ach, enough of this!" Rory tried a shaky laugh. "We'll both be greeting like weans if we're not careful." He paused. "Let's get to the meat of it. Now that I'm walking around a wee bit, Josh Mason and I have come up with a plan."

Callum hardly dared to anticipate where Rory's words were going.

"Josh has spoken to some of the other settlers, and they are all keen for the school to start; they can spare their sons and daughters until the end of March, when we hope for good weather. Josh's son Seth has finally convinced his father that he's never going to be a scholar and that he wants nothing to do with schooling, so he's volunteered to help me until I'm fit to work on my own. That way, we can free you to take up schoolmastering. What do you say to that, young Callum?"

Rory was almost bowled backward as Callum threw his arms around his neck. "I would love that dearly, Uncle," he said, then stopped, worried that Rory might take his words the wrong way. "I didnae mean," he said, "that I hate it here, or anything."

"It's all right, laddie. I know you're no farmer, but I could do with your help in the summers, till Sandy's big enough to do a man's work."

"You'll have it, Uncle Rory. I promise."

Callum could not remember when he had felt so happy, when it had seemed that everything was right with his world. It was a strange happiness, though, one tinged with sadness, as Callum realized that he was no longer drifting, tossed by circumstances. Callum was in control of where life would take him and how it would serve him.

Dog shifted in the doorway, trying to find a more comfortable position.

Rory laughed. "Oh, Callum, what am I going to do with you? Making such grand promises. But I know you'll try to keep them." Rory got to his feet, leaning heavily on Callum's shoulder for support. "Let's go and tell your aunt that you've agreed to our plan, although I think she would be more surprised if you hadn't."

Callum stood, too, and hugged Rory once more, as hard as he could. "I'll finish up here, Uncle. I'd like to think awhile, if that's all right with you?"

"Aye, laddie, you do that." Rory maneuvered his way past Dog, who rose as if to follow him.

"Dog, wait. Stay and keep me company." Callum's fingers strayed to his pocket, where the box was stowed. He felt the broken wood, which he had never repaired, despite his intention.

Dog stared reproachfully at him and sat down with a thump, her eyes fixed on the woods that were fading into the darkness of night.

Callum sat back on his heels and produced the box, holding it just under Dog's muzzle. She gave no sign that she saw anything. Callum placed the box delicately on the ground between Dog's front paws and then moved backward until he stood against the cow's stall. He could feel the cow's sweet breath on the back of his neck and reached up absently to pat her drumlike flank, as he began to cry.

Dog's lips peeled back from her teeth and she used them to carefully tease the contents out of the box. She held it for a moment, then with a whiplike movement, threw it into the air, where it writhed and shimmered. It hurt Callum's eyes to look at it, so he covered them with his hands. When he looked up, the girl from the woods sat on the floor by the doorway, regarding him steadily with Dog's calm brown eyes. Her long black hair cloaked her body. She sat with arms clasped around her drawn-up knees. In one hand, she held a wisp of midnight fur.

Callum forced himself to breathe deeply before he spoke. There was a wariness about the girl, like that of a wild creature who would bolt at any sudden movement. "Who ... what are you?" Callum's words were muffled by his tears.

A half smile twisted the girl's mouth. "I am Dog and I am me," she said in a voice husky from disuse.

Callum tried once more. "The man who sold you, who was he? Had he imprisoned you?"

Her face contorted with distaste. The girl spat on the ground. When she spoke it was in a harsh, grating whisper. "My brother, but not my brother now." Raising her head, she sniffed the cold night air just as Dog was wont to do. She looked hard at him, then she threw back her head and bayed. Dog's silvery howl floated out above the trees. An answering howl came back, deeper and distant.

The girl smiled at Callum sadly. "He is near. I must go now. My grandfather has been searching for me for a long time." She stood up, stretching her arms and legs to ease their cramps. Callum started as if to stop her, but she made a gesture with her fingers and he found that he was sitting down again. Stepping lightly out of the barn, she moved into the clearing, stopping halfway across and turning. "Farewell, Callum Murdoch," she said. "I am Dog and I am Airah." With that, she set off once more, only to stop again as if something had just occurred to her. A broad smile on her face, Airah said, "Enjoy your freedom, Callum, and always treasure him who gave it you." She started to run then with great easy strides.

As she neared the trees, Airah threw the dog skin into the air. Its color was hidden by the night sky, but Callum saw what looked like a sparkling net grow until it enfolded her. Dog loped into the darkness, carrying something between her teeth.

Darkness had filled the barn. Callum rested his head on his knees, unsure whether his tears were born of sadness or joy.

Epilogue

The sun shone brightly. A cool breeze ruffled the leaves that glowed with a fresh, new green. Callum shouldered his box and whistled. The innkeeper, Eli, had offered him a ride back to his uncle's farm, but he had chosen to walk, wanting to enjoy the pleasant airs of spring. He also thought he might make a detour to Mason's farm and see Amy, who, on one of her trips to town, had promised to bake him a pie. He licked his lips and sighed. For all that she was young, Amy Mason could outcook women twice her age.

As Callum walked, he thought about what was waiting for him: Rory hale and hearty again, and raring to clear more land. Callum looked ruefully down at his hands. By the end of summer, the palms would be like leather from wielding the ax if Rory had anything to do with it. Still, he could not complain — once the harvest was in, he would return to town and the school. He smiled, thinking of the number of pupils already promised for next year. It had been hard at first; some of his pupils had not enjoyed their lessons — the first schooling they had ever had — and made their restlessness very clear. It had taken all of Callum's patience and artifice to make his lessons engaging. The fiction of Mr. Swift had proved invaluable, the amusing tale of Gulliver entrancing them all. So, he smiled, the school must be counted a success.

A flickering movement caught Callum's eye. Racing through the trees alongside the road, like a black silk ribbon, was a dog. In the distance, ahead of him, he saw the tall raw-boned figure of an old man. He started to trot and then ran as fast as he could toward him. Amy would happily feed them all.